W9-API-958

For Dianne;
And for Little Flower;
Welcome to the club.

SCP

For my friends and lovers,
my mom and brother,
and especially my collaborator
who taught me much of art and craft;
Thanks, Dad.

SDP

ALIENS™

BOOK THREE
THE FEMALE WAR

Steve Perry & Stephani Perry

(Based on the Twentieth Century Fox motion pictures, the designs of
H. R. Giger, and the graphic novel by Mark Verheiden and Sam Kieth.)

A DARK HORSE SCIENCE FICTION NOVEL

Aliens™ © 1992 by Twentieth Century Fox Film Corporation.
All rights reserved.™ Indicates a trademark of
Twentieth Century Fox Film Corporation.

BANTAM BOOKS
NEW YORK · TORONTO · LONDON · SYDNEY · AUCKLAND

ALIENS: THE FEMALE WAR
A Bantam Book / August 1993

All rights reserved.
Copyright © 1993 by Twentieth Century Fox Film Corporation.
Aliens™ copyright © 1992 by Twentieth Century Fox Film Corporation.
Cover art copyright © 1993 by David Dorman.

No part of this book may be reproduced or transmitted in any
form or by any means, electronic or mechanical, including
photocopying, recording, or by any information storage and
retrieval system, without permission in writing from the publisher.
For information address: Bantam Books.

If you purchased this book without a cover you should be aware that this
book is stolen property. It was reported as "unsold and destroyed" to the
publisher and neither the author nor the publisher has received any payment
for this "stripped book."

ISBN 0-553-56159-6

Published simultaneously in the United States and Canada

Bantam Books are published by Bantam Books, a division of Random House, Inc.
It's trademark, consisting of the words "Bantam Books" and the portrayal of a
rooster, is Registered in U.S. Patent and Trademark Office and in other countries.
Marca Registrada. Bantam Books, New York, New York.

PRINTED IN THE UNITED STATES OF AMERICA

OPM 19 18 17 16 15

**Don't miss any of these exciting *Aliens,
Predator,* and *Aliens vs. Predator* adventures
from Bantam Books!**

Aliens #1: Earth Hive by Steve Perry
Aliens #2: Nightmare Asylum by Steve Perry
Aliens #3: The Female War by Steve Perry
and Stephani Perry

Aliens: Alien Harvest by Robert Sheckley

Aliens vs. Predator: Prey by Steve Perry
and Stephani Perry
Aliens vs. Predator: Hunter's Planet by David Bischoff
Aliens vs. Predator: War by S. D. Perry

Predator: Concrete Jungle by Nathan Archer
Predator: Cold War by Nathan Archer
Predator: Big Game by Sandy Schofield

ONE ON ONE

RIPLEY fell into the shallow water, grunted and jumped up into a crouch. She tried to look in all directions at once, managed one; there was no immediate danger.

She didn't believe that the drones would have left their queen unprotected, but the only motion around her was the gently swaying ocean.

Doesn't mean it's going to stay that way . . .

All of her senses were in overdrive. The putrid odor of the planet, combined with the heat and gravity made her dizzy. Along with the fading sound of the APC, there was only the slosh of the water against her legs. The fierce winds had suddenly dwindled to almost nothing.

An alien's cry echoed through the dead air, but it came from the direction of the retreating transport.

She turned and faced the cluster of nests.

"It's just you and me now," she said.

"If you are captured by the Indians, don't let them give you to the women."

> Attributed to U.S. frontier cavalrymen during the attempted extermination of the Dakota Sioux.

1

Ripley felt the little girl's arms tighten around her neck as she slammed the lift button repeatedly.

The queen was almost certainly right behind them. They were going to die down here. The thought filled her with a sudden dizzying wave of sickness and she hit the button again. They were going to die in this hellish, humid, artificial pit on a crumbling planet, a big piece of which was itself about to be blown into atomic dust.

"Come *on*, goddammit!"

She hiked the crying child up higher and looked back over her shoulder into the darkness. Steam hissed from a ruptured pipe, adding a hot fog to the dankness of the alien-spittle covering the walls. She could feel it coming, could almost hear the rapid steps of the approaching mother, even over the screaming alarms and sirens. She had destroyed its children, hundreds of its deadly offspring, and she had no doubt that it was on its way to rip her and the girl apart.

She looked up then, saw the bottom of the lift slowly descending, still a few floors up. Any second now . . .

From behind them came a piercing scream, inhuman, full of rage. Ripley instinctively clutched her weapon tighter and ran to the ladder attached to the wall; maybe they could catch the elevator on the next level up. "Hold on to me!" she shouted.

And then *she* was there, like the others but larger, swollen even if no longer gravid.

The queen had a huge crown, a comb of glossy black that swept up and back from her misshapen head. A second set of arms, smaller, jutted from her chest. It—*she*—moved slowly toward them from around the corner a few meters away, hissing and drooling.

Ripley backed away; the girl tightened her small, sweaty hands in a finger lock to keep from falling.

The lift, it was here!

Ripley spun.

The door opened, the mesh gate slid away, and they jumped in. Ripley slapped the control button more frantically than before—

The queen ran toward them—

The wire gate closed . . .

Shut a second before the alien got there.

Ripley put the girl down, pointed her flame-thrower at the creature, fired through the mesh. The fuel was low; only thin and weak spurts of flame came out, but it was enough to stop the alien.

The queen snarled; thick streams of slime dripped from her open jaws. She held back.

The outer door closed.

Safe! They were safe!

The ride up was rough; explosions rocked the building, falling pieces of debris slammed into their all-too-slowly-rising lift. But they made it to the flight deck.

As the outer door opened, a calm female voice informed them that they had two minutes to get the minimum safe distance from the site, before the whole processing plant blew itself into non-existence. They ran together from the lift, and—

Where the fuck was the ship?!

It was gone! Their ride had taken off; that god-damned *machine*, the android, had betrayed them!

Ripley screamed in anger, pulled the little girl toward her. Flames leaped all around, the building rocked and shook with deafening noise ... and now, another sound. Ripley looked at the lifts.

Another elevator coming up.

Oh, no. It couldn't be. The queen couldn't know how to operate an elevator! She *couldn't*!

But she is smart, a little voice said inside Ripley's head. You saw her when she realized you were going to burn her eggs, how she waved the drones off, kept them away from you. At first.

Ripley looked at her carbine. The counter said it was out of ammo. The flame-thrower taped to the gun was also dry. She dropped the weapon, picked up the child, backed away.

The lift came to a stop, the door slid open. Ripley hugged the girl tightly.

"Close your eyes, baby," she said, and closed her own.

"Ripley? Are you okay?"

Ripley opened her eyes and looked at Billie, the young woman sitting across from her. Billie looked concerned, a slight frown creasing her brow. Ripley liked her, had liked her in the first moment or so of meeting—unusual. Trust was hard to come by these days, at least for her. But Billie's account of her childhood rescue had stirred up some stories of Ripley's own. . . .

"Yeah," she said, and then sighed. "Sorry. I got lost there for a minute. Anyway, the last thing I really remember is settling into sleep after LV-426, me and one of the soldiers and a civilian, a little girl. I—I guess the ship must have sustained some damage somewhere along the way. I don't remember anything else. I woke up in a crowd of refugees on Earth six weeks ago, and they were on their way here; it seemed like a good idea—everything was falling to shit down there. So I've only been here a month longer than you have."

Billie nodded. "So what did the medics say about the missing part? Physical or psych damage?"

"I don't do medics," she said, smiling a little. "Besides, I feel fine."

Ripley stood and stretched her arms over her head. "Want to walk with me to dinner?"

Billie glanced curiously at the older woman as they headed toward the cafeteria. She was the first survivor, so far as anyone knew, to have seen the aliens and gone back for more. Billie found herself intrigued by Ripley's relaxed, confident demeanor, a calmness that seemed unlikely after all she must have been through. Especially given her own experiences with the monsters. Even after only two weeks here, it seemed like a million years had passed.

They walked down C-corridor toward the nearest dining hall. There was a viewing plate adjacent to the hatchway that led them down another corridor; peering out the window was a young couple, both medtechs by the look of their IDs, holding hands and talking quietly. Billie saw one whole stretch of the station from her vantage point, long tubes set into spheres and cubes, assembled like a giant child's toy. She shivered slightly from the cold as they neared the hatch. The station was made from heavy plastic and cheap lunar metals; heat came from baseboard heaters set along each corridor, but the void outside kept the corridors from ever really getting warm.

Apparently the newer modules were worse, exposed plastic beams and cramped quarters with poor facilities and lights. They had been slapped together to field the incoming refugees from Earth, the flood of people that had finally tapered to a trickle. Gateway Orbital Station now held somewhere around 17,000, almost twice the number it had been intended for—but it wouldn't need to hold many more. As Ripley said, things were falling to shit down there.

Though it was early for dinner, the hall was crowded. There had been a midday shipment of real vegetables from one of the hydroponic gardens, and word had spread fast.

Billie and Ripley both got small salads of carrot and lettuce to go with their meals. They sat at one of the smaller tables near the entrance. In spite of the crowd, it was quiet; most of the people on Gateway had lost friends and family to the aliens on Earth. It was almost like people were embarrassed to laugh or have a good time. Billie could understand that.

She had spent much of her life in various psych wards, trying to convince medtechs that the aliens existed; the solemn atmosphere of the station was familiar, if not comforting. She didn't feel particularly at home here, but then she'd never really had a home. At least her life wasn't in danger; that was something. After the trip with Wilks, being safe seemed almost like a dream.

Ripley ate a bite of her heated soypro and made a face. "Tastes like insulation that's been dehydrated, frozen, and reheated. Then spit on."

Billie tasted her own, then nodded. "At least it's warm."

They ate quietly, each concentrating on her meal.

"So do you dream of her? The mother alien?"

Billie looked up from her tray, startled.

Ripley watched her intently. "*I* do," she continued. "At least I did, before my memory lapse." She took another bite of soypro.

"I—yeah. I do, too. I've heard that others have dreams. . . ." Billie trailed off. Yeah, she had heard stories, mostly about fanatics, people who had turned their dreams of the aliens into some kind of religion; the Chosen who had realized that Judgment Day had already come. She'd mostly kept quiet about her own dreams, but recently . . . "I have them often. Almost every night."

Ripley nodded. "It got that way with me, too. They started with her reaching out, expressing love, and turned into these. I felt a connection. They were transmissions. I knew where she was, that she wanted to gather her children to her. The queen of the queens, the driving force behind the whole goddamned species. I knew where to *find* her!"

She pushed her tray aside abruptly. "And I lost her."

Billie nodded. "I knew I wasn't the only one, but I haven't had a lot of time to think about it lately and this station doesn't offer a whole lot in the way of group therapy sessions."

Ripley smiled, a short, bitter expression. "I think I know what she's waiting for," she said, "and I have an idea. We need to find more dreamers . . . what about Wilks?"

Billie shrugged. "I know he dreams, but I don't think it's the same way I do. That doesn't mean much. He keeps to himself. We could ask him." She glanced around, although she figured he had gone for a workout. In their two weeks at the station, Wilks had spent most of his time in some gym or another. "I'm supposed to meet him later for a drink."

"I'd like to come along—if it's not intruding," Ripley said. It seemed she chose her words with care.

"No problem. You're welcome." Billie smiled, and Ripley smiled back, a much easier expression than before. Billie found herself liking this woman more and more.

Wilks had been cycling for the better part of an hour, working up a real good sweat, when he noticed the young boy sitting in the corner with his head resting on his hands. He had been concentrating on the vid screen in front of him, a level-nine cycle run that was going to make him hurt like hell tomorrow, or he might have seen the boy earlier.

It was one of the station's smaller gyms, and he liked it that way; the larger workout rooms could hold 200, and that many people sweating in one place wasn't particularly appealing, especially given the smell of recycled air. And he didn't care much for crowds.

The kid was maybe ten or eleven, a thin, pale boy with dark hair and a neutral expression. He stared at nothing, his chin resting on his knees.

Something about him reminded Wilks of himself at that age; maybe it was the build or the hair ... maybe the blankness. He could relate to that.

Wilks had grown up in a small town on Earth in the southern United States, raised by his aunt; his mother had died of breast cancer when he was five, after his father had left the two of them the year before. Aunt Carrie was nice enough, but didn't spend much time with him; she worked the night shift at a rest home and was rather indifferent to his life. Little Davey Arthur Wilks had enough to eat and clothes to wear, and that was her responsibility as she saw it, that and nothing else.

Carrie Greene did not understand much of anything, and sure as hell not little boys.

They didn't discuss his parents often; his mother was a saint who had nothing but love for Davey, his father a no-account bastard son of a bitch who had nothing but his own best interests at heart. David—who hated being called "Davey"—wasn't so sure. He couldn't really remember either of them, and although he knew his mother wasn't gonna come back, he did dream of his father coming to get him one day, standing on their weather-beaten porch with a smile for his son and things to play with and a new place to live. His dad was handsome and strong and smart and didn't take shit from *nobody*.

It was late summer, two days after his eleventh birthday. David lay on the floor of their small, stuffy living room with his newest Danno Kruise,

Action-Man comic. Danno was in the middle of kicking some serious bad-guy butt when there was a knock at the door. Aunt Carrie was "resting her eyes" in the back bedroom, so David answered, expecting a salesman.

A tall man holding a brightly wrapped box stood there.

"David?" The guy was badly in need of a shave and wore a shabby suit a few years out of date, the synlin frayed at the cuffs.

"Yeah, why?" David stepped back from the door a little; he didn't know this man. This man with bright blue eyes . . .

"Ah—well, hi. I knew it was your birthday, and—well, I was in town. Here." The stranger pushed the box toward him.

David took it and looked at him. "Who are you?"

"Oh, hell." The stranger smiled weakly. "I'm Ben. I am—was a friend of your mother's." Ben looked at his watch, then back at David. "Happy birthday, Davey. Listen, I gotta get going, I'm supposed to meet someone . . . you know how it is." He looked at David helplessly.

David stared, unable to speak. His *father's* name was Ben. He clutched the package tightly. The wrapping crinkled under his grip. Ben.

The man turned and walked away, without looking back. David stood there for a long time before he closed the door. He tried to tell himself that it wasn't true, that this Ben wasn't his dad. It couldn't be. He wouldn't just come here, drop this present off, and *leave*. He wouldn't do that.

"Davey?" His aunt, risen from her nap, padded toward him. "Was that somebody at the door? What have you got there?"

The boy stared at her. He shook his head. "It wasn't anybody important," he said. He tossed the present at the shiny copper ash bucket his aunt kept next to the antique wood stove.

In the gym, Wilks shook his head again. Jesus. Some of those old tapes were real fucking hard to get rid of. He stared at the boy. "Hey, kid, you won't build any muscle sitting on your butt like that."

The boy looked at him, like some kind of big-eyed bird.

"Here. Let me show you how that machine works."

It wasn't much, but it was something Wilks could do. Nobody had ever done it for him.

The smile on the boy's face was worth a million, easy. And it didn't cost Wilks anything at all.

2

Amy and the old man stood in front of a tunnel covered in alien secretion and littered with debris. The tunnel led off into thick darkness.

The old man ran a shaky hand through his dirty white hair and put his arm around the adolescent. Amy smiled up at him. She was a pretty girl, in spite of her grimy skin and tattered clothes. Her nervous smile made her look much younger.

"They're using the underground to move beneath the city," he said, keeping his voice quiet. "The tunnels and grids are still here, but changed. Transformed." He and Amy walked forward a few steps. The lighting was weak; long shadows danced and re-formed beyond them as they moved through the silent cavern.

The old man continued:

"It's—it's difficult to be sure, but the tunnels appear to converge into a central locus—like spokes on a wheel."

The dark, ropy alien construct surrounded them completely now. The walls were embedded with long-dead humans—a mostly rotted arm hanging down from above, a half skull jutting out to their left. To the right was something that might have been a dog once.

Amy moved closer to the old man.

"As far as I can tell, the creatures keep to one area at a time, use it up, and move to another. Our camp is set up nearby." He put a shaky hand on Amy's shoulder. "The aliens are a few klicks from here, as far as I can tell, so we're as safe as we can be."

"I wish we could go up," Amy said. "We can't, though."

The old man nodded. "There are those who feel the 'connection' and hunt for alien breeders above ground. We're better off down here."

They walked down through the tunnel, death all around them like obscene art, both breathing shallowly through their mouths. After a minute they stopped, and the old man began to speak again in his schoolteacher's voice.

"We're not far from the hub now, one of the central areas. That's why there are more breeders here, what's left of them. We don't dare go any farther."

Amy shuddered slightly. "Can we get out of here, Daddy? It doesn't feel right."

He looked around warily and then smiled at the child. "Yeah, okay. Let's get an early dinner." They turned back to the tunnel, the old man letting Amy take the lead.

"You know, I should've—" he began, when suddenly a hand shot out from the dark wall and grabbed his knee. Amy let out a single, high-pitched yelp. The old man fell.

Another voice came out of the darkness. "Oh, shit. Oh, *shit*!" A young man ran into view.

"Paul!" shouted the old man, and the younger one ran to help him. "Get it off me, get it off!"

Paul held a small lantern into the air over the old man. A breeder was strung into the black secretion there, close to death. It had once been a woman, and now was barely animal, its eyes insane. It held tight.

"Daddy," Amy breathed out, chest hitching. She started to sob.

Both Paul and the old man beat at the woman's hand with their fists, but she would not let go. Her face was bloated and almost black. Paul looked toward the hub; somewhere, maybe far away, there were clattering noises.

"Lisssen," she rasped out, her lips bleeding and cracked. "I am the mother . . ."

Paul stood and kicked at her hand. The thing's wrist snapped cleanly, and the old man scuttled backward, away from the dying creature. She didn't seem to notice that her hand was hanging off her wrist; she didn't seem to feel pain.

The old man stood, grabbed Amy by the arm, and they all backed away from the mad breeder.

She closed her awful eyes. "Soon," she whispered hoarsely. "Soon, soon." The terror was there on all of their faces as they moved back toward camp, her final words seeming to echo all around the trio.

The old man said, "Paul?"

The younger man nodded. "I'll take care of it." He pulled a knife from a sheath on his belt. A stray beam of light glittered from the blade. He moved back toward the breeder—

The screen went to static. Billie found her hands clamped to the arms of the chair so hard her tendons creaked when she managed to loosen her grip. She shook her head back and forth, almost without realizing that she was doing it. A denial of Amy's pain, of her own—

She was in Gateway's main broadcast room, alone; the tech had gone on his dinner break.

"Not again," she said, feeling like a little girl herself. Her own childhood of running and hiding on Rim had never seemed closer—everyone gone, dragged away screaming to be food for the creatures. A flood of memories hit her: crouched in a ventilation duct while a fat man with bleeding ears howled in fear and pain a few feet away; gunshots and shouts in the middle of the night; blood splattered in the dark hallways; and always the terror, the constant, aching terror and hopelessness, the certainty that she would be discovered by the monsters. And eaten. Or worse.

But Amy was alive! A few years older and still alive.

The tech, an elderly man named Boyd, had mentioned offhand that there were still a few things coming in from Earth. "Mostly those goddamn religious shitheads," he'd muttered, picking at one ear.

"Any 'casts of a family?" said Billie, not expecting it. That would have been a miracle. . . .

"Oh yeah. Comes in on various channels, pretty random signals. A girl and her dad, couple of others off and on. Sad."

Boyd had shrugged and left to eat, warning her not to touch anything while he was gone. Billie figured the old tech hadn't meant he didn't care, it was just that there was nothing to be done. Except—

Ripley. Maybe her plan, whatever it was, could mean helping Amy. The same child, now older, she had seen in the 'casts when she and Wilks had been trapped on that mad military asshole's base. Amy.

Billie took a deep breath and let it out slowly. She saw herself in that little girl on Earth and would do whatever she could to save her. Anything.

Billie was a few minutes late to the Four Sails, no doubt the sleaziest bar on Gateway—and of course the one that Wilks *would* come to. It was small and dark. Drinkers and chem-heads sat at round tables surrounding the tiny stage near the back; according to a schedule posted on the wall, there would be erotic dancers later, couples and threesomes crowded onto the platform performing to pulsing music.

Billie spotted Ripley by herself at a table in the corner, a pitcher of splash and a few glasses in front of her.

"Wilks isn't here yet," Ripley said, pouring pale straw-colored liquid into one of the glasses. "Drink?"

"Yeah, thanks," said Billie. She took the glass. She swallowed half of its contents before setting it down.

Ripley raised an eyebrow. "Hard day?"

"Some of my past catching up to me. There's a family on Earth that sends broadcasts out—I first saw them on Spears's planetoid. One of them is a little girl, maybe twelve or thirteen now. Watching is—" Billie stopped and sipped her splash. "It's hard."

"Is it Amy?"

Billie looked up, surprised.

Ripley said, "I saw one a few days ago. Do you know her?"

Billie shook her head. "I feel like I do."

"Yeah, I understand. Amy was my daughter's name, too." She drank.

Wilks stepped through the doorway, nodded to the bartender, and came to their table.

"Sorry I'm late," he said. "I was—uh, weight-training. Guess I lost track of time." He smiled and sat down, then poured himself a glass of splash.

Billie noticed that he seemed much more relaxed than usual, his scarred face almost calm.

" 'Lo, Ripley."

Ripley leaned forward. "We need some help, Wilks," she said. "No point in coating it—do you dream of the aliens?"

"Doesn't everybody?" he said.

"Not nightmares," Billie said, her voice quiet. "Signals. Transmissions. From a queen mother, a leader of queens. She's—she's in a dark place, a cave or something, and she *wants*. She's waiting, she's calling."

Billie closed her eyes, remembering. "She moves closer, and then she speaks. She says she loves you and wants you with her; you can feel it coming off of her in waves, her need . . ."

Billie opened her eyes. Ripley was nodding. Wilks wore a skeptical look.

"Maybe it's something you ate," he said.

"Listen, Wilks, remember the robot ship? The dream I had?"

Wilks nodded. "Yeah. I remember."

Billie had known there were aliens on that ship when there was no way she could have; that dream had saved their lives.

"So what do you want from me?"

"We need to know who's having dreams," said Ripley. "I had 'em for a while, but they stopped; if they're actually transmissions of some kind, we may be able to use them. But we have to find out if anybody else dreams them to be sure. Any ideas?"

Wilks stared into his splash. "Maybe. I can ask

some people I know. If you think it's really worth doing."

"I don't know if it is," Ripley said. "But it might be."

Wilks shrugged. "Fuck it." He took a big drink of his splash. "Not like I got a whole hell of a lot else to do on this bucket of rocks and plastic. What the hell. I'll ask around." He drained his glass. Stood. "Meet you in the B-2 conference room at 0900 tomorrow."

Ripley smiled and Billie let out a deep breath, relieved. Amy was still hiding on Earth, and there was probably nothing she could do; but they were going to do *something*.

The private conference room was military access only, but it was small and rarely used, so Wilks had no trouble signing it out. Ripley and Billie stood on either side of him in front of a small computer. He spoke as he tapped in codes.

"I looked up an old friend last night, Leslie Elliot. She used to go out with this guy I trained with, till she realized that she had about 50 IQ points on him. She's a pretty good hacker, but these days she's doing basic data entry. I figured she wouldn't mind rascaling up what we needed ... she even edited. Wait, here we go."

A readout scrolled up the screen. Names, dates, places. Then vid images.

Quincy Gaunt, Ph.D./Subject: Nancy Zetter. It was a poor quality vid of two people sitting in an office, the woman speaking:

"... and then she comes up to me and I hear

this voice in my head telling me that she cares about me. She says, 'I love you.'" The attractive middle-aged woman shook her head, disgusted. "That awful thing, telling me that."

"And that's where it ends?" said the doctor, a thin young man with a neutral expression.

"Yes. Except it *doesn't* end," she said. "I keep having them—"

Wilks pushed a button on the console. More names blipped across the screen, another office with different people. A well-built young man squirmed nervously in a cushioned chair while an older man looked on.

"It's like—I don't know, she *wants* me," he blurted out.

"Sexually?"

The young man colored visibly. "No, not like that. Like—aw, shit, I don't know, like she's my mother or something."

"Do you dream about your mother?" said the doctor, leaning forward.

Wilks hit a button. A Dr. Torchin was talking to a female Lieutenant Adcox.

". . . and you feel like she's calling you to come be with her in these dreams," Torchin said. "Interesting."

Wilks handled the keyboard swiftly.

". . . it's a recurring dream—"

". . . she loves me, wants me—"

". . . you say the creature is asking you to find it—"

"It wants me to find her—"

". . . she's calling me—"

Wilks hit the stop button and turned to look at the two women.

"How many?" said Billie, her mouth dry.

"Not sure," said Wilks. "But Les accessed a week of psych visits and she came up with thirty-seven."

"And there are a lot of people who don't go to psych," said Ripley. She looked thoughtful. "Good job, Wilks."

"Where the fuck is this headed, Ripley?" he said, leaning back in his chair. "Does this mean something?"

"That queen mother wants her children," said Ripley. "I don't know why she wants them, but she does. The signal is for them. The drones aren't smart enough to load themselves onto starships and fly home. But if we could find her, get her to Earth—"

"They would go to her," said Billie.

"Lemme get this straight: This queen of queens is in another *stellar* system? Christ, you're talking faster-than-light transmission of this fucking call. Voodoo stuff."

"But what if it's true?" Billie said. "What if somehow the superqueen *can* make that long-distance call? Think how it would work if she were here."

"They would head for her like lemmings," Ripley said. "Gather themselves in a big bunch all together, every one of them."

Wilks wasn't the brightest guy who ever lived, but he saw the possibilities of this scenario pretty damned fast. When he spoke, his voice was soft, but interested: "We could wait until they all got collected into a big bunch and then nuke 'em all to hell."

He looked back at the vid screen, where a patient with dark circles beneath her eyes was frozen in mid-sentence. Nice dream, but that's all it seemed to be. He'd drifted since his first contact with the monsters, lost a big chunk of time, until he'd rediscovered Billie in that psych ward, and a new purpose along with her: to destroy the aliens who had fucked up him—and mankind—royally. That was his goal, but he was a practical man.

To Ripley, he said, "What makes you so sure about this?"

She shook her head. "I'm not sure, at least not in any way you could lay out and measure with a rule or a scale."

"But you believe all this psych stuff means what you said? There's some kind of supermom alien somewhere who could draw these bastards like shit does flies?"

"That's what I believe, yeah."

Wilks stared at the screen. Billie had been able to tell about the aliens on the ship he and Bueller and she had stolen, that was a fact. And he'd had his own hunches, ducked when there wasn't any reason to do it, and saved his ass because of it. He wasn't much on religion or psyche stuff, but you didn't have to be a chemical engineer to start a fire, either. Pragmatic was the way to go, to hell with the theoretical crap. If Billie could dream the truth, maybe other people could do it too. Made sense.

"Okay. Let's suppose this scenario works," he said. "It's worth checking out a little more. If it's right, it gives us a big hammer we can use against the suckers. I'm willing to play along and see where it goes. I'll go talk to my friend."

"I'll go with you, if that's okay," said Ripley. "Billie? If you could dig through these files, pull out names of military personnel—"

Billie plucked the metal info sphere out of the reader and put it in her pocket.

Ripley grinned. "Fine. Why don't we meet this evening and see what we've got?"

Billie walked toward her quarters quickly. It was good to be in action, better to know that she shared her dreams with others, that she wasn't alone. Ripley was a strong woman, a leader.

She turned a corner and almost ran into a robotech adjusting a light panel. Billie stopped short and stood there, studying the design. It was simple machinery, made for only a few manual tasks; vaguely humanoid, about two meters tall. Basically a control box with arms and legs.

Not like an android that you could mistake for human . . .

Billie was suddenly very near tears. Mitch. She wondered what had become of him, her android lover. As always, a mix of confused emotions came with the thought: anger, that he hadn't told her the truth; worry, sadness. The pity she had felt when he'd been "repaired" on Spears's plane-toid, his lovely torso strapped to ugly metal legs— like the limbs of the robot moving past her. When the final realization had hit, it had been too late; she and Wilks were in space, headed away from the battle on the planetoid where Mitch had been trapped. The transmission to their ship was the last she had seen of him. The truth of it was that for whatever Mitch had come to be, he was the best person she had ever known. And she had loved him.

Yeah, okay, so, life was fucking unfair. It was a cold fact that she'd learned and relearned too many times to cry about now. You spent a lot of time in a hospital, you learned to suck it up and keep your face blank.

Billie wiped the tears from her face. Crying didn't get you anywhere. If she'd learned nothing else in her recent adventures with Wilks, she had learned that the best way to get things done was to do them. You wanted an ass kicked, best you wore your heavy boots. Then you could take care of business. Sitting around and whining didn't get it done.

Ripley knew. Ripley had a plan. What the plan was didn't matter as much as the fact that it existed. And if there was any chance at all that it would work, Billie was going to help make the damned aliens suffer for what they'd done.

And laugh while they burned.

3

Ripley rubbed at her temples, frowned slightly.

"Problem?" Wilks whispered. He didn't want to disturb the woman concentrating at the console a couple of meters away.

"Headache," she said. "I get 'em a lot lately." She gave up her self-massage and looked around the small cubicle. The tasteful paintings and prints seemed out of place next to the cheap, built-in furnishings.

The tech, Leslie Elliot, had agreed to help them, volunteering her lunch break to dig for their information. They sat now in her cube, watching her work. She was an attractive woman, tightly muscled, with an easy smile and reddish-brown hair that she wore in tiny braids. Ripley wondered how well she and Wilks were acquainted. . . .

"Maybe you should stop by medical," said Wilks, interrupting her thought.

Ripley looked at him blankly.

"Your headache."

"Oh. No. I'm fine. Besides, I don't do medics; most problems seem to fix themselves."

Wilks seemed about to say something else when Leslie turned in her chair and grinned. "You owe me for this, Sarge," she said.

"If you got something."

Leslie's grin widened. "Gold mine, what I got. Just gotta ask the right questions. Hold on a sec. Gotta store these where we can find them and nobody will stumble across 'em."

Ripley smiled at Wilks.

"Okay, so maybe you aren't totally crazy," he said.

Ripley and Wilks walked toward Ripley's quarters. The smell of canned air seemed particularly stale in this corridor, a metallic tang that you could almost taste.

Wilks thought about the conversation they'd just had with Les.

"Only a few of the dreamers seem to be linear-minded," Leslie had said, tapping the keys expertly as she talked. "You know, math-science, left-brain types. Guys like you, Sarge, no imagination."

"Fuck you."

"You wish. Um, anyway, it stands to reason that

they would have a better fix on charting a map. If you'd told me what you were looking for last night, you could have saved yourselves a trip."

"Actually, we're making this up as we go along," Ripley said.

Even so, they had the names of people who could describe the alien's planet, six in all. Their details were vague, but Leslie had cross-referenced a known-systems map and come up with several possible locations. Ripley said she figured they could narrow it down if they could talk to the six.

This telepathy-empathy stuff was tricky, but it was what they had to work with. Wilks was still willing to go along for the ride, given that something had turned up. Weird, but there it was.

"I thought we blew their goddamn planet out of space," Wilks said. "I dropped chain-linked nukes that should have scraped the fucking surface clean."

"Doesn't matter," said Ripley. "They spawn wherever they are, and a planet overrun is a planet overrun."

"Yeah. But this one, wherever it is, appears to be the core. Makes me wonder how many places are seeded ..." He trailed off, remembering the conversation with the old soldier in the bar.

"Something?" Ripley said.

"Yeah. A few days after Billie and I got here I met this old man at the bar, name of Crane. He was ex-military and very drunk, wanted to buy every uniform in the place a drink. He rambled, glory days and dead soldiers, shit like that, I didn't pay much attention—until he started talking about the aliens. He called them war toys; said that they were too good at surviving to be natural."

Ripley turned to look at Wilks.

"Interesting," she said, considering for a minute. "Rapid procreative ability, acid blood, vacuum-resistant—it would explain a hell of a lot if it were *designed* that way."

Wilks nodded. "Worth thinking about, anyway. 'Course then the questions get worse: Who designed the fucking things? Why? What do they have in mind?"

They stopped in front of Ripley's quarters. "I'll catch up to you and Billie later," he said. "I've got some things to check out."

Ripley shut the door and thought about Wilks's secondhand theory. War toys? What insane species could've come up with the alien design; what kind of war could have warranted it?

Her headache was coming back.

There was a knock at Ripley's door.

"Come in."

Billie stepped in and glanced around at the bare walls of the older woman's room. Efficient and practical, like Ripley, who sat at a desk staring at the console in front of her. She looked weary.

"Hey, Billie," she said, swiveling in her chair. "Anything?"

"Eighteen military-affiliated, maybe half of

them trained in combat," she said. She leaned on the desk. She was on the tired side herself.

"Good. Wilks and I got some stuff from his hacker friend that looks promising, so we can get started. We'll have to do background checks on some of these folks and get going on transport—sooner the better."

Billie smiled at Ripley's straightforward confidence in her plan. Must be nice to be so in control, so sure of yourself. "Just out of curiosity," she said, "how did this idea of yours come up?"

Ripley shifted in the chair and looked suddenly uncomfortable. "You remember I said I had a daughter?"

Billie nodded.

"Amanda. She was very young when I left to work on the *Nostromo*. I promised her I'd come back for her birthday. I didn't make it."

Billie nodded again. She knew that part of it. Ripley had spent decades in deep sleep—she held the record, as far as anybody knew. It had been a lucky accident that she had been found at all, drifting through dead space. Billie wondered what it must have been like, to leave a child and come back to find she had died as an old woman. A daughter older than your own grandmother. Awful.

"On the ship to Gateway, I thought a lot about her, her whole life passing by while I slept. And the dreams of another mother who wanted her children back."

Ripley shook her head and smiled. There was no humor in the expression. "Funny comparison.

Me and that monstrous creature both wishing for the same thing."

Billie needed to do something. Awkwardly, she reached out and took Ripley's hand. "I'm sorry," she said.

"Yeah." Ripley pulled her hand away, not accepting the gesture of comfort. "Anyway. I didn't have any kind of revelation about what to do, no brilliant inspiration. I just loved my daughter and I miss her and I blame that *thing* for taking her away."

She looked up at Billie, her eyes angry. "My idea didn't come from wanting to save anyone, no great love for humanity—I just hate her and her whole fucking brood and I want them *exterminated*."

She took a deep breath and dropped her gaze, then shrugged. "Enough history. We have a lot to do."

Billie wondered how old the child had been; Amy's age, perhaps? Something that all three of them had in common, then; Ripley, Billie, and the alien queen. Just wanting their children ... No. Amy wasn't her child. Just a face on a viewscreen. Don't think of her that way.

Billie moved a chair over to Ripley's desk and sat beside her. There would be time to sort through the reasons later. For now, Ripley was right—there was a lot of work to be done. After two weeks of hanging around, the idea didn't seem so bad. Doing nothing was always worse than doing just about anything.

4

Sergeant Kegan Bako was ten years younger than Wilks and looked years younger than that. He had a baby face and a blond's complexion, fair and unwrinkled. Wilks guessed that Bako only had to shave every other day, if that, to keep with military office standard.

The two men sat in Bako's office, separated by a desk covered with paper flimsies and plastic food wrappers. The small room was stuffy, the smell of soy sauce cloying in the air.

"Sure you don't want some of this? Better than that shit they serve in the dining rooms." Bako maneuvered his chopsticks clumsily to his mouth, losing at least half of his fried noodles in the process.

"Thanks, I already ate some of the dining room shit."

"Too bad. So what brings you here? Don't tell me you're looking for a rematch—?"

"What, you haven't suffered enough this week?" He'd met the younger man at a gym while looking for a handball partner. They'd played several times since; although Bako hadn't won yet, it was a good workout and okay company. "Actually, I wanted to check something. Who'd I talk with to requisition a transport?"

Bako swallowed a mouthful of noodles and grinned. "God, maybe. You're kidding, right?"

"Hypothetically, let's say I wanted to go pick up a . . . weapon that might wipe out the infestation on Earth. Could I get a ship?"

"What kind of weapon?"

"A hypothetical one."

Bako tapped his chopsticks against the desk. "Well, first of all, you'd have to have proof of this weapon, no hypothetical about it. Take that to General Peters, or maybe Davison—get an okay, a volunteer crew, and fill out the forms." Bako made another attempt at his noodles as he spoke. "I gotta tell you, though, you'll have a fuck of a time, even with solid evidence."

"Why's that?"

"In the last four months there have been three attempts to get to and from Earth. Three *official* attempts, if you know what I mean."

Wilks nodded. That meant other times that nobody wanted to talk about.

"The first ship came back with a dozen or so

new civilians but four marines outright dead or gone out of an eight-man crew. On the second, we lost almost all the crew and got zip rescues to show for it."

"And the third?"

"Didn't come back. It's like the things knew the ships were coming and were laying for them. And we really can't afford to lose any more hardware, local manufacturing facilities being what they are. Just about every crate that could get free of the gravity well left during the final days of the infestation. Some of those ships are here; a whole shitload more of them are far away, and nobody knows where."

Bako set his chopsticks down and looked at Wilks. "They're planning another mission soon; you know how the brass hates to have its butt kicked, although you didn't hear it from me. My point is, getting a ship to do something that could *maybe* help isn't high priority right now. Even scout ships are worth more than diamonds these days."

And all Wilks wanted was a fully loaded starship to take God knew where across the galaxy to kidnap the mother of all aliens. Hypothetically speaking.

He nodded, stood, and smiled at the baby-faced sergeant. "Thanks, Dimples. You've been a help."

"Don't call me that. C-court tomorrow, 0800?"

"Sure. I'll tie both hands behind my back, even things up a little."

Wilks exited on Bako's laugh, but stopped smiling as the door closed behind him. Bako's information hadn't exactly been a surprise. And if it were just him, he'd fuck going through the proper channels and just take a ship. He'd done that and he knew how it worked. But he didn't exactly live in a void. Someone else was in charge, and if Ripley wanted to try and go by the book, he'd do what he could to help. But unless the general was dreaming of the alien superqueen, proving anything was going to be a bitch.

Charlene Adcox answered her door wearing a pale green kimono tied loosely at the waist. She was short and almost boyishly thin. Her close-cropped hair and sharp features made her look oddly masculine in spite of the gown she wore. Billie caught a scent of perfume, light and flowery.

"Fem Adcox?"

"Yes."

"My name is Billie. Could I speak to you for a moment?"

"Concerning . . . ?" Adcox smiled politely.

Billie took a deep breath. "It's about the dreams," she said.

Adcox paused, then moved back from the door, her smile gone.

Billie stepped in. The room was larger than her own, decorated with Japanese prints and sparse, simple furniture. Adcox motioned to a futon for Billie to sit down, and seated herself across from her on a small wooden bench.

"How did you get my name?"

Billie hesitated. The psych files were classified,

but an elaborate lie would eventually be found out by anyone whose help they enlisted. "There are others having the same dream," she said. "Some of us rascaled the psychiatric files."

Adcox nodded. "Okay," she said. The young lieutenant seemed more relieved than anything else, which Billie understood. "How many others?"

"We can't tell for sure. Upwards of fifty, at least. They're all the same—they're transmissions, not dreams. The aliens are telepathic or empathic, whatever. It ain't coincidence."

Adcox offered her a weak smile. "No, it doesn't sound like it. What do you want from me?"

Billie pulled an info sphere from her pocket. "You can tell me where you think she is," she said. "There are several possibilities described in these files. Only a few of us seem to be able to see location in the dreams, and you're one of them. We want to find her."

Adcox tensed slightly. "To kill her?"

"Yes. Her and her children."

Adcox reached out and took the sphere from Billie. "Call me Char," she said.

Ripley wrapped the towel around her neck and padded naked to her bed. She stretched her long body across the pad, toes pointing and arms over her head. The interview with John Chin had gone well. He was an architect, one of the linear-minded dreamers, and had agreed to look at their map. Chin wasn't a fighting man, and she doubted he would volunteer to come with them when the time came—but she imagined that there would be enough soldiers willing to take the risks. . . .

She closed her eyes. She wasn't sleepy, but the shower had relaxed her to a meditative frame of mind. She wondered how Billie had made out with Lieutenant Adcox ... how old was Billie? Twenty-three, wasn't it?

In October of Ripley's twenty-third year, she had given birth to a beautiful, squalling, perfect little girl, Amanda Tei. Amy ...

Ripley let her mind fall deeper into the memory.

"Shhhh, Amanda. Little sweet Amanda." She repeated the words over and over, a soft, lulling mantra to the newborn she held. The hospital room was dimly lit and done in soft colors. She had never met, and would never meet, the father; she had gone to a clinic, safer and neater for her single life. Except now she was a mommy. . . .

When the nurse laid the tiny child in her arms, Ripley had wept. She was so beautiful, so quiet and sleepy and tiny! Perfect little fingers and nails, a headful of dark, silky hair.

The labor had been hard and long, but it was worth it.

"Shh, little baby, sweet Amanda," she crooned, wondering how she could ever show her daughter how much she loved her, with this love that could move mountains. . . .

A man's face suddenly appeared a few inches from her own, frowning, his hand reaching out to touch her—

• • •

Ripley yelped, sat up in bed, eyes wide. She covered herself with the towel and looked around the room. No one. But—that face, that was—

The man's face had been in her head, in her daydream. And it had been—

"Bishop?" Ripley shook her head. The android, the one with the soldiers, *decades* after her daughter had been born, years after her mother had failed to get home in time for her birthday.

Where had *that* come from? Bishop ... she hadn't thought of him for a long time; the last time was—she had seen him last—

No good. Her pleasant wanderings had gotten weird somewhere; maybe the strain of everything was getting to be too much to handle. Ripley sighed, confused and frustrated by her inability to know her own mind. Maybe she was tired after all. . . .

Ripley stood and reached for a coverall. She didn't feel like being naked anymore.

5

Wilks tapped on Leslie's door using the small bottle of whiskey he'd bought.

"Hold on a sec!"

He heard muffled footsteps coming toward him, and then a loud thump. "Shit!"

Wilks smiled. The door opened to a very red-faced Leslie rubbing her right knee. Behind her was an overturned chair.

"Wilks, you asshole," she said, straightening up. She wore a snug black bodysuit and matching headband; sweat dotted her tawny skin. In spite of her words, she grinned. "That for me?" She motioned at the bottle.

"Well, if you're busy—"

"Depends."

"I wanted to thank you for helping us out; thought we might have a drink, unless you're otherwise involved—?"

Leslie grinned wider and stepped back from the door. "You always were the subtle type," she said, and her voice softened slightly. "Come in, David."

Billie sat in the uncomfortable plastic chair and watched the vid screen flicker with the ruins of Earth. The scanner roamed, and it surprised her how much old data was still being broadcast. Mostly advertising for companies long dead, sometimes documentaries, the occasional fiction program; many were in different languages. Billie touched the command button from time to time, looking for something real, something current.

Something like Amy.

There was a flash of static and then a black screen. Suddenly a man's face appeared, a close-up. Middle-aged, he was handsome in a rugged way, sharp nose and strong jaw dominated by intense, dark eyes. His mouth was tightly set, deep lines etching the corners. He stared into the camera as if he were about to fight it, his gaze unwavering. Something about the bland determination on his face reminded Billie of—

"This is an exercise of faith," he said. "Of the new Christ and the power She commands." His voice was deep and compelling.

Spears, she thought. Like Spears.

The camera pulled back to show the man standing on a low platform in a poorly lit studio. He was tall and short-haired and wore a tight coverall that emphasized his biceps and chest. A large knife was strapped to one hip.

"I am Carter Dane," he said, "and I have seen the Truth."

Billie heard quiet murmurs of approval from offscreen.

"There is power in my hands. The Goddess has shown me the way."

He began to pace back and forth as he spoke. "The Goddess brings no fear. The Goddess has no fear. We are Her children, She our mother. We are not worthy of Her; it is the failing of humanity."

More mumbles of assent.

Dane continued, his voice rising. "When the cleansing began, I was afraid. I cried in self-pity and *fear*—afraid for my own life and the lives of the weak and unworthy all around me." He paused, for dramatic effect. "I was no more than a pile of shit," he said.

"Yes!" A hoarse cry from the unseen audience.

"Useless and impotent fear," he continued, "left me empty. Incapable of action. I *wallowed* in it; I was *crippled* by it!" He stopped moving, faced the listeners.

"And She spoke to me. She asked for my help. The Goddess, the creator of so much power, asking a cripple to aid Her. Like She asks of all Her Chosen. And I became *strong* for Her, I learned of Her love, I found that death is *shit*! It is *fear*! It is *nothing*!"

Billie sat transfixed, watching the screen; she

found herself unable to move, to hit the command button. Another of the dreamers, and completely insane.

Dane motioned to one side and a heavyset woman in ill-fitting soldier's gear dragged a young man onto the stage. His hands were tied behind him and his slow, stumbling movements suggested heavy sedation. The soldier pushed him to the floor next to Dane and stepped back into the shadows. The boy looked barely out of his teens, was thin and dressed in rags and dirt. He lay on his side, eyes closed.

Dane pointed at the prisoner but kept his gaze on the listeners. "This," he said with disgust, "is humanity. Weak. Afraid. He is not fit to be the giver of Divine life, not when so many of the willing stand strong and proud in front of me." Dane made a sweeping gesture toward the crowd, and put his hand on his hip.

Put his hand on the hilt of the knife.

He pulled it out slowly and held it up. "The old humanity has outlived its usefulness," he said.

He knelt beside the boy. The youth gave no sign of having heard the speech and did not struggle as Dane pushed the blade without apparent effort deep into the bound boy's throat.

Blood erupted out across the platform.

The boy opened his eyes and his mouth, as if to speak. A horrible, wet gurgle was all that came out, a look of confused pain on his pale face. He rolled onto his back, his eyes fluttering. More blood spewed from the wound to mat his dark hair and white skin. His thin body shuddered in one final spasm. His eyes remained open.

Dane ran the back of the knife across his forehead, smearing red across his brow. Swiftly he ran the point of the blade from the groin to the sternum of the dead youth, cutting deeply. He turned to face his listeners, a wild grin on his face.

"Come and feed!" he shouted. "Eat of the flesh! Devour the old, become one with the Goddess!" He dropped the knife to the floor and thrust one bloodied hand into the boy's gut, then lifted it to his own mouth. Dark figures stepped onto the stage, tattered men and women converging on the corpse, a dozen or more, faces crazed, laughing loudly, reaching, pulling—

Dane ranted on, his mouth dripping blood, his voice cracking. "We are the Chosen! We will become! We will—"

Billie hit the command button convulsively, breaking the trance. The screen went to static and dimly, as if from another place, she heard a commercial for a retirement complex begin. She shivered all over. She stood, knocked over her chair. She ran blindly away from the madness, her hand over her mouth. There was a waste bin in the corner of the room; she stumbled to it and vomited. Retched again and again.

Slowly her surroundings came back into focus. Her spasms subsided into hitching, ragged breaths. "Okay," she said, "okay, okay." She brushed at her watering eyes. The dreams had been too much for their minds to bear on top of watching their world crumble, their families killed. But not her. They were sick, demented; she was here, and would change things.

"Okay," she said again, and straightened up. The smell of vomit was overpowering and sour, and she stepped away from the bin. She felt a sudden fury at what the queen had done. Her and her goddamn calling, urging those people into madness. Giving the unbalanced a reason to kill . . .

Billie sniffled and wiped her mouth with the back of one shaky hand, then took a deep breath. The boy's dying face would come back to her later, she knew; there was nothing she could do to change that. For now, she would concentrate on what she *could* change.

Wilks gently cupped his hand over one of Leslie's soft, small breasts; she stretched leisurely and covered his hand with her own, smiling.

They lay nude in a tangle of sweaty sheets, the musk of recent sex in the air. Wilks propped himself on one elbow beside her. He felt relaxed and at peace with his body. Leslie was a good lover, confident in her abilities without being assuming.

"Mmm," she said, and opened her eyes to look at him. "Not bad, Sarge. You should be promoted."

Wilks smiled. "Yeah, I think I make a pretty good drill sergeant. Drill, drill, drill . . ."

Leslie made a face. "On the other hand, your jokes leave something to be desired. Like humor."

"What? Hey, I'm funny."

"Sheeit."

They lay still for a moment, preoccupied with their own thoughts.

Wilks remembered his conversation with Bako. The evidence of the mother queen's existence was not overwhelming in his own mind, so proving it to somebody who didn't know Billie—specifically, to the general—would take a lot more than what they had.

"When are you leaving, David?"

"Hmm?"

"The dream alien. You're going to wherever she is. To get her."

It was a statement, not a question.

"I don't know," he said. "There's still a question of how—official backing is iffy." He shook his head. "We're not even sure of where she is yet. Ask me when I know more."

"And you're going with nothing more solid than a psychic vision?"

"Less—I don't even dream the dream. But you do. Do you believe it?"

"Yeah, I think she's real." She nuzzled her head against his bare chest. "I'll do whatever I can to help."

Wilks stroked the palm of his hand across her smooth belly in small circles, then moved lower, lightly touching the edge of her pubic mound. "Yeah? Anything?"

She pushed up against him, eyes closed. His penis stirred, pressed against her leg. She rolled toward him, a sly smile raising a corner of her parted lips.

"You *are* pretty good as a drill sergeant," she said. "Now which is for shooting and which is for fun . . . ?"

Alone in her quarters, Ripley shut down the computer and rolled her head forward, yawning. Her thoughts had started running into each other. It was late and the pills she had swallowed for an earlier headache didn't seem to be working. Stronger medication would require a prescription, and her intrinsic mistrust of medtechs—

She frowned. How had that come about, anyway? Must have happened after the long sleep, some incident in the hospital that had lodged in her subconscious. She couldn't recall caring either way before that. . . .

It didn't really matter; headaches were not a major problem. Besides, it was most likely the stress of getting this action together that caused them.

She felt satisfied that they had their planet. Both of the dreamers she and Billie had talked to had fingered the same system, and Leslie had listed it as the most probable.

She walked to the bed, knuckled her tired eyes, and lay down, not bothering to undress. She hadn't seen Wilks for a while and wondered if he had gotten the information about military transport. It would be best to get the go from the power on Gateway, but if they couldn't—well, there were other ways.

She thought about the daydream she had experienced earlier, of Bishop's face surprising her back to reality. She had liked the android, an exception to her negative feelings for synthetics—but his appearance in her mind had seemed wrong. Out of place, not of her own memory.

Medtechs and artificial humans, the world of science and personal demons. Maybe they were all crazy. Maybe the idea was nothing more than a madwoman's nightmare and Ripley had stumbled into it. Maybe ...

Ripley fell asleep.

Peter Schell was a heavy-
set older man whose natural expression was a
slight scowl; even when he smiled his brow
creased downward. Ripley thought he looked like
he had bitten into something sour.

The man next to him, Keith Dunston, was
much younger, around Billie's age. He was small-
boned and wiry, a martial arts teacher. Dunston
had listened to Wilks outline the situation with a
placid interest, as if he were watching a 'cast of a
tennis match.

Ripley had let Wilks do most of the talking to
the two men. They had met in the private dojo
where Dunston taught classes. After brief intro-
ductions, Wilks had quickly laid out their theory
and research; Schell had interrupted several

times with questions while Dunston remained silent, occasionally running a small hand through his short red hair. Both men looked tired.

"So what if you don't get a transport?" said Schell.

Wilks shrugged. "Right now we're trying to get a crew. The more people who have faith in this, the better the chance we *will* get a ship."

"Yeah, but what if you don't?"

Schell's open skepticism was getting on Ripley's nerves. She didn't think he was going to end up working on this. . . .

Wilks took that one: "We'll burn that bridge when we come to it. Any more questions?"

There was a moment of silence. Wilks glanced at Ripley and back to the two men, who sat thinking.

Schell scowled at his watch. He stood and reached out to shake hands with Wilks.

"I appreciate your inviting me to this discussion. The dreams will be easier to live with knowing what you've told me—but I'll have to think about it and get back to you."

Wilks started to say something, but must have thought better of it; he shook hands with Schell.

Schell nodded at Ripley and Dunston, and exited.

Ripley sighed. Not everyone they spoke to was going to jump at the chance to risk their lives, of course.

"I'm in," Dunston said.

Ripley looked over at the man, surprised. He

had been so quiet through the presentation that she had guessed he wasn't interested.

Dunston didn't look as if he had said anything important; he sat with the same unreadable expression on his unlined face. "Let me know what I can do to help you prepare."

Wilks and Ripley both grinned. The sergeant explained the proposal they planned to give to General Peters. Ripley watched Dunston absorb the information. The teacher seemed to radiate calmness and strength; he would be a good man to have with them.

Billie sat on Char Adcox's futon and sipped a mug of black tea, waiting for her response. The lieutenant had seemed enthusiastic enough at the beginning of Billie's speech, but now looked apprehensive; she tapped her fingers against her own cup, frowning. Billie remained quiet, not wanting to pressure her.

"I don't know," Char said finally. "It sounds good, but I'm not really in a position—" She hesitated. "I had family on Earth," she said. "It's taken me a long time to deal with losing them, and I've worked hard to get where I am now as it is. Some mornings, I'm still barely able to get out of bed." She looked at Billie, searched her face for understanding.

Billie nodded.

"I just don't ... look, I can't, I'm sorry."

Billie tried not to look disappointed, but it must have shown.

Char sipped her tea, her eyes troubled. Billie

set her mug down and stood to go. "It's okay, Char," she said. "Really. We couldn't have gotten this far without your help. I understand."

Billie walked to the door. Damn. She liked the lieutenant, had been certain that she would volunteer.

She turned. "If you change your mind . . ."

Char nodded, but her forced smile said that her decision was firm. Billie walked out and stood in the corridor for a moment. She shook her head. She did understand. Given that the last couple of weeks had been the only time she'd been able to catch her breath since Wilks had come back into her life, she could see how peace and quiet had a lot of appeal. Then again, she realized she'd spent too much of her life in an enforced peace and quiet to want to sit still very long. Even if there were monsters out there waiting for her.

"Well, McQuade is in," Wilks said. "And Brewster. Did you get to Falk?"

Ripley nodded. "Yeah, but he lost interest when the question of payment came up. He said he'd *consider* it if we wanted to buy his time."

Wilks shrugged. "Not everyone has cause," he said. Too bad, though. He had run into Falk a few times on the station. Tall and heavily muscled, he was one of those guys whose loud voice and laugh could be heard in the midst of every card game. Not a real social adept, maybe, but he had the feel of somebody who'd be good to have covering your ass in a firefight.

They sat in Ripley's room, going over possible

crew members. McQuade, Brewster, Dunston, and Jones so far. Jon Jones was a young medic who seemed too serious for his age. Ripley had seemed tense when Wilks had mentioned the black doctor, but had not objected. A medtech would be a necessity, they both knew that.

Billie had stopped by earlier to say that Adcox wouldn't be going. She had seemed unhappy about it and hadn't stayed to discuss the trip. Wilks guessed that she was at the 'casting room looking for Amy; it had become an obsession of hers, looking for Amy. He understood why.

"What about Carvey? And Moto, she's had experience—"

Wilks returned his attention to the screen. A light flashed in the upper corner, accompanied by a muted tone, signaling a call.

Ripley tapped the receiver. It was Billie.

"Ripley, Wilks," she said, her voice strained, "tune in military channel, ten-vee, quick!" She discommed before either of them had a chance to reply.

Ripley hit the controls that would switch them to vid.

The image on the screen was confused, jumbled; Wilks recognized the inside of an armored personnel carrier. A pair of legs from the knees down ran by, then another set; apparently, the camera was on the floor. There were shouts and gunfire in the background. A man's voice, near hysteria, called out orders that were barely audible above the din.

"Broillet, Reiter, fall back! Hornoff, Anders,

Sites, respond! Respond! Fuck! There's no—" the voice was cut off.

Wilks started. Hornoff was one of the men listed in the psych files. . . .

There was nothing on the screen now except a dim shot of a storage compartment. The picture jerked slightly, as if the APC were being hit. Occasional bursts of gunfire could be heard in the distance, but no more voices.

"What—?" Ripley glanced at Wilks and looked back to the picture. Her expression was part dread and part anger; she knew what she was watching, if not the circumstances.

"Earth mission," said Wilks tightly. His knuckles were white. Bako had said there was going to be another.

"Old 'cast?"

"I don't think so. I was going to look up Hornoff tomorrow." He watched realization flood Ripley's face. She chewed at her lower lip. There was no reason for this to be on, unless—

"Somebody fucked up," he said.

Suddenly there came an alien's hoarse shriek, loud enough that it had to be inside the APC. There was no sound of a weapon to answer its cry.

A thick, spidery shape moved across the screen, too close to see clearly—but Wilks knew.

Ripley groaned. "Oh, shit."

The screen cut to static, then black. Neither of them said anything for a moment, just watched the darkness. A mechanical, unisex voice chimed on, informing them that there were technical difficulties.

"It was a mistake," said Wilks. The 'cast had played for less than two minutes, if Billie had caught the beginning; the voice meant that it had been pulled on purpose. Ten-vee was a consistently boring channel dedicated to pro-military information programs, propaganda. He could almost see some vidtech private sweating in his boots right now. A colossal fuck-up. The wrong tape switched to at the wrong time; everyone on Gateway tuned in would have seen it.

A harried-looking man stepped on to the screen and faced the camera. His brow and upper lip were dotted with sweat. His face and hair looked military, but he was dressed in a rumpled coverall.

"It's weasel time," said Wilks softly.

"You're *on*," a voice stage-whispered offscreen. Live, of course.

"We, uh, apologize for the interruption in regular programming," he said. "Due to an error in our video room, a transmission of the . . . Earth mission from five weeks ago was . . . put on." The PR man fumbled his way through a rationalization, obviously unprepared.

"What bullshit," Wilks said. "No way that was ever supposed to see air."

"We now return to, ah, the program. Ten-vee will issue a formal statement at a later time." The screen cut to a space walk, some minor fix-it operation on the station. Ripley hit the command, blacking the picture. She turned to Wilks, her face pale and numb.

"Won't people know?"

Wilks shook his head. "Maybe friends of the dead soldiers. But who will they talk to before command gets to them?" He realized his hands were still in fists and let them relax, taking a deep breath. "This was supposed to be a secret, and they're going to step on it hard. Believe that."

Ripley looked at him. "What do you think this is going to do to our mission?"

Wilks returned her look, frowning. What *would* it do? The military couldn't keep people from talking . . . it could swing the transport problem either way.

"I don't know," he said. "I guess we'll find out soon enough."

Billie was getting ready for bed when her 'com *chinged*. She almost ignored it; whoever it was would try back at another time. She was exhausted and it was very late—she had gone back to the 'casting room after meeting with Wilks and Ripley and watched for Amy for another few hours.

All three of them had agreed it was an accident; someone had their ass in a sling by now for that little technical error. She *had* caught the beginning of the transmission and had called the others within ten seconds; they hadn't really missed anything, except the camera hitting the floor.

Billie sighed and stretched. There had been no

sign of Amy, and now someone was calling in the middle of the night.

She hit receive. "Yes?"

"Billie? This is Char Adcox. I didn't wake you, did I? I'm sorry to be calling so late—"

Billie felt her sleepiness slip away. "No, I was up. What's going on?"

"Did you see the ten-vee fubar this afternoon?"

"Yeah, I saw it."

Adcox sounded exhausted, too. "I've been thinking about what I saw. It brought back a lot of history—I'm sure it did for others—" She stopped, then laughed weakly at herself. "I'm sorry, I'm kind of a mess."

"You don't have to apologize, Char, it's fine."

There was a pause at the other end so long that Billie was about to speak again, when she heard the lieutenant take a deep breath. "I want to go with you," she said. Any trace of hesitation was gone. "If you still want me along, that is. I—need to go."

This was the voice of the woman she had seen on the tape of the psych files, strong and unafraid. "Good. Welcome aboard."

They made arrangements for the next day and discommed.

Billie lay down to try to sleep. She instinctively liked and trusted Char Adcox, and was happy the woman would be coming along. And having one of the linear dreamers on board wouldn't hurt.

Billie drifted off to a deep sleep. If the queen mother haunted her dreams, the next morning brought no memory of it.

7

Ripley opened her door and found Falk standing there, his face solemn. He had one hand raised to knock and dropped it; the big man looked as if he had slept badly. He smelled of stale alcohol and sour sweat.

"Falk," she said, "what a treat. I was just on my way to breakfast."

She saw that the sarcasm in her voice didn't escape him. He reddened slightly. "Yeah. Well, I wanted to talk to you for a minute, I—about the trip. I want to go."

Ripley stepped back, surprised. Falk obviously took it as an invitation; he walked over to the desk and leaned against it. He kept his gaze on the floor.

She looked him up and down. He had been sitting when she had met him the day before and she hadn't realized how huge the man was. At least 195 centimeters and 100 kilos, barrel-chested and long-legged. His receding hair was worn long in a blond ponytail, his mustache was slightly darker. Embarrassment didn't rest well on his hard face, and he looked as if it were an unfamiliar emotion; one corner of his mouth twitched, and his heavy brows were drawn together.

"We aren't offering money," she said finally.

His expression didn't change. "Yeah, that's fine. You still need help, don't you? I'm sorry I was such an asshole. I want to go."

Ripley frowned. This wasn't the man she had met yesterday, the loud, wise-cracking, up-yours pirate. He had admitted to having the dreams easily enough but treated them lightly. He said his woman had insisted on the psych visits and he had called them a waste of time.

"Why?" she said.

Falk sighed and looked up, but not at Ripley. "The military channel," he said, focusing his attention on the ceiling. "You heard about their little fuck-up yesterday?"

"I saw it."

"I was in the middle of a card game at a bar when it played. I almost had to beat the shit out of the 'tender to turn it up—" He seemed out of breath and paused for a few seconds.

Ripley waited.

"Marla was one of those soldiers," he said. "She told me that she would be gone a while, said it was standard drill shit. She told me not to worry."

Falk finally looked at Ripley. She saw that his eyes were bloodshot and rimmed in red. "Last night some asshole dressed in a captain's uniform told me that there had been an 'unfortunate accident' on her ship and that it'd be a good idea for me to keep quiet about it. The bastard stood there and *lied* to me; I heard her name on that 'cast, I heard somebody yelling it—"

Falk stopped and took a shuddery breath. All of Ripley's earlier dislike for the man evaporated. He was obviously in great pain.

"I'm sorry," she said, "I wish there was something I could do...."

"I want to go," said Falk. "I want to kill them." He didn't sound angry or desperate; his voice was calm and matter-of-fact, as if he were discussing the weather. "I loved her."

"We're meeting at 0800 tomorrow in the dojo on C," she said.

He straightened up at that and nodded, his expression unreadable. Ripley understood what it was like to lose someone close and knew there was nothing she could do to make it easier for him.

"Thanks," he said, walking to the door. "I'll be there."

She had no doubts about that.

Wilks watched General Peters scan the printout sheet of the psych files Leslie had pulled. To avoid problems with confidentiality and computer rascaling, she had only included the names of the dreamers they had spoken to, along with statements from Billie and Ripley; twelve in all. Ten of them had agreed to go.

"And you say that this dream is the same in all of these cases, Sergeant?" The general spoke without looking up.

"Yes, sir." Wilks stood in his office at ease, hands behind his back. It was one of the more palatial rooms on Gateway, well-lit and comfortably warm. Pastel paintings were hung on the walls and the stuffed chairs were a high-quality synthetic leather. Peters had not asked him to sit.

The general had not gotten as far as he had through imaginative thinking. His stoic expression and hard eyes said as much—standard military right down the line. The man was also quite fat, hadn't seen much hands-on combat lately. Wilks had served under such men before, assholes too closed-minded and by-the-numbers to believe in anything outside their own experience. He was wasting his fucking time here, but Ripley wanted to give it a shot. Fine ...

"Well, this is very interesting," Peters said, looking up, "but I'm afraid there's really no way I can authorize such a trip on just this. We'll have to look into it further." His tone was dismissive.

Wilks said, "Is there somebody else I can speak to about this, sir?"

"Excuse me?"

Wilks shrugged. He was still a marine, sort of. They hadn't been able to pull all his records, so his status was pretty much in limbo until they did.

That gave him a little leeway when talking to officers. He said, "Well, sir, there are civilians in the
governing board. They might be interested in
this."

Peters looked at Wilks with his piggy eyes.
"Are you trying to be smart, Sergeant?"

"No, sir." Not with this clown. Say something
smart and it would sail right past.

"Yes, there are civilians in power here, but
when it comes to military missions using *my hardware*, I am *God*."

Wilks said nothing, waiting.

"I've read your record, Sergeant, and you've
got a long history of being a troublemaker. I don't
need any more trouble than I've got." Peters set
the proposal aside and motioned toward the door.

Wilks could see that there was no chance. If he
thought kissing ass here would work, well, fuck,
he'd done worse, but he knew it was a waste of
time. Had known it all along, but at least he'd held
his temper in check. There was a time when he
would have popped fatso here right in the mouth
and smiled as he waited for the MPs to come get
him.

"Thank you for your time, sir."

The general grunted but didn't look up from
his desk, where he was already looking through
other papers.

The temptation to slam the door on the way out
was one that Wilks was only barely able to resist.

Billie met Wilks at the Four Sails. He sat at his
table staring at his drink, his scarred face tense.

"Ripley 'commed, said she'd be a few minutes late," said Billie, and sat down. "How'd it go with the general?"

"About like I expected. Head was jammed too far up his ass for him to begin to hear me." He sipped at his drink. "Fucking officers."

Billie felt her stomach clutch at itself. This had become important to her. How could she get to Amy, how could she still hope that the child would be alive?

"What's the matter with you two?" Ripley said. She slid into the booth and sat across from them. "Are we ready for our meeting tomorrow?"

Wilks said, "Yeah, if we can fly without a ship. The general thinks we're crazy. No surprise."

Billie's heart felt heavy. "It looks like the game is over," she said. "Unless you want to *steal* a ship."

Ripley grinned. "I thought you'd never ask," she said.

Wilks returned the grin. "I knew it. I fucking knew it."

"You didn't really think some fat old general was going to *give* us a ship, did you? That was a long shot at best."

Wilks nodded. "Gonna make us criminals again."

"Well, sure, it would've been nice, but we don't always get what we want, do we? Time to go to plan B," Ripley said. "Which was really plan A all along: We swipe what we need."

"Makes sense to me," Wilks said. He raised his glass in salute. "Here's to crime."

Billie smiled and nodded. Well. It wasn't as if they'd never done it before. Christ, they were getting to be old hands at stealing ships. The one from Earth to Spears's military base, the one from there to here, the escape pod. It did make sense. What the hell.

What the hell.

8

Wilks looked over the group they had assembled and nodded. Everyone here had field experience, with the exceptions of Jones, the medic, and Dunston—although he taught hand-to-hand combat in the dojo where they all now stood or sat in small groups, talking. And Dunston looked as if he knew how to handle himself.

Brewster, Carvey, Moto, Adcox, and Captain McQuade were all marines and had fought on Earth at the beginning of the infestation.

Ana Moto was a thin, sad-looking woman with long features and a bright laugh. She was also the only surviving member of a special task force assigned to spot alien nests on Earth before things had gotten bad. She laughed at something Adcox

said to her and Billie; the three young women
stood together in one corner of the room.

Everyone had arrived early, with the exception
of Falk, who walked into the dojo exactly on time.
Ripley hadn't mentioned why he had changed his
mind, just that he would be coming after all.

Wilks watched Falk nod at Ripley when he en-
tered, and noted that the big man looked exhausted. He suspected that Falk had decided to
go after watching the military 'cast, and figured
that he had known one of the soldiers. Just a
hunch. Falk sat apart from the others in one of
the plastic chairs and stared at the scuffed foam
floor. He looked like a man in pain.

Leslie smiled at him from across the room,
where she was talking to Ripley and Maria Tully,
a friend of hers. Tully was skilled with computers
and had lost family on Earth; she would be the
electronics tech.

Wilks had mixed emotions about Leslie. On the
one hand, he wouldn't have minded having her
along, for personal reasons. On the other hand,
his expectations of surviving the mission weren't
all that high. Ultimately he was glad she wasn't
going; he didn't want anything to happen to her.

Wilks smiled back at her. After meeting with
Billie and Ripley in the bar, he had gone to
Leslie's quarters to discuss her part in their mission. Although she wouldn't be making the trip,
her role would still be a major one in helping
them get transport.

The room grew quiet as Ripley walked to the
front to stand next to him. Billie left her group to

join them, although they had both agreed to let Ripley run the session; she was a natural leader, and it was her idea anyhow. Wilks was glad somebody else was in charge for a change. Made things easier on him.

"Well," she began, "you all know why you're here. I'm Ellen Ripley, this is Wilks and Billie. Each of you has had certain useful experience, which is why you among the dreamers have been chosen. You have felt the alien presence, the queen—and it's time we did something about it."

Ripley had everyone's full attention; Wilks hoped that they'd still be listening after they heard the bad news.

"Before we work on the specifics of our mission, we need to let you know some of the obstacles we're looking at here. Wilks?"

He cleared his throat. "Yeah. I talked to General Peters yesterday, and he refused our request for transport." He paused. "Actually, the man thinks we're bugfuck."

Captain McQuade broke in. "Peters is an asshole," he said. The two marines with him nodded. "I'm surprised you bothered—the man's so full of shit he farts instead of burping."

Several people laughed.

Wilks grinned. "Yeah, well, be that as it may, we don't have the official green light. We can try again, but I think the general is a waste of time."

Ripley took over. "Which is why we've decided to borrow a ship," she said, "and that makes this an entirely different game. I want you all to understand what you're agreeing to before you make a

final decision. If we get caught, we're in deep. If
we fail, coming back here means consequences—
maybe even if we succeed."

She met the eyes of each person as she spoke.
"We didn't tell Peters where we were headed specifically, so we probably won't be chased if we get
clear—but stealing a transport wasn't part of the
plan when you agreed to go, and if you want to
walk, now's the time. We'll understand."

There was a pause.

"Fuck it," said Falk from the back of the room
in a hoarse voice. "Not doing anything would be
worse."

There were several murmured affirmations
from the group.

Wilks looked around the dojo and saw the
same kind of determined look on everyone's face.
No one moved.

After a moment, Ripley went on. "Good.
Thanks. We want to leave here in a few days, and
there's a lot to do to get ready. We're looking at
ships now, and Leslie"—Ripley nodded at the
hacker—"is getting us a read on the security system we're dealing with. We've got a list of shit
that needs to be thought out, supplies and weapons to begin with, and we need to work out
details of taking the ship. . . ."

As Ripley continued, Wilks watched the expressions of the people they would be working with.
Several of them threw out suggestions as the discussion continued, and all of them looked as
though they had been bestowed a special privi-
lege in being included on this trip—this trip that

could cost them their lives and probably would.
Yeah, they were a good crew.

Not too bright, maybe, but he didn't have any
room to talk.

Billie checked the supply list for the third time,
cross-referenced with what was stocked on the
Kurtz. The military freighter had been chosen for
its large hold, designed to haul toxic liquid by-
products. The containment area could hold up to
10,000 cubic liters of radioactive sludge, was airtight, had interleaved durasteel-and-lead walls half
a meter thick, with hatches to match. Anyway, the
hold was more than big enough to carry a queen
alien. And to keep her from wandering around the
ship, too. If they could catch her, if they could get
her on board, *if* they could steal the ship in the
first place. . . .

Billie rubbed her eyes and looked around her
room. It was late; she knew she should get some
sleep. In the morning they would meet back in
the dojo to run down the details of taking the
ship. Security looked to be minimal, but there was
some, and they didn't want to get caught.

She and Doc Jones had been put in charge of
provisions, although the list Leslie had rascaled
seemed pretty complete. The *Kurtz* was built to
quarter twenty people comfortably; it carried an
APC and the food dispensers were stocked with
pastes and concentrates that would be good for
another ten years. "Good" being a relative term;
they would taste like shit, but they would be edi-
ble. The ship was currently fueled and ready to

go. All the comforts of home. More than she had here, actually.

In spite of her exhaustion, Billie felt too wired to sleep. Her thoughts were a jumbled mess of memories and hopes, all that she had been through and the people she had known. As awful as the dreams that she had experienced at the hospital on Earth had been, they were even worse these days. Wilks. Mitch. Now Ripley. And, of course, Amy.

It seemed to Billie she had been running and fighting her whole life. She was in a place where she didn't have to do that anymore; she could probably live out her life here on this station and maybe die of old age. But that thought didn't play. There were people down on Earth being eaten alive and that wasn't right. Especially since one of those at risk was Amy.

So, maybe she could go and do this thing and somehow survive, and maybe *that* would be the end of it.

Amy. The *Kurtz* probably wouldn't be equipped to receive Earth 'casts at the distance they would travel, so there would be no way to know if Amy and her family were still alive. The last transmission had been only a few days before, but there was no way to know if it had been on tape or live; Billie wanted to believe it was recent. She could feel that Amy was down there, perhaps praying for a way out.

Ripley's plan would be the answer.

Billie scanned back to the top of the list, yawned. She knew that there was nothing missing, but wanted to check once more. After all, there would be no second chance—when they got on board, there was no turning back.

Hell. It was already too late to turn back.

Ripley sat on the floor of the dimly lit dojo, alone. It was early morning. The crew wouldn't arrive for another half hour and then there would be no time to think.

She knew that they had planned the mission as thoroughly as possible, that they were as ready as they would be. They could probably spend another day or two working out details, but one could always wait; it was time to act. Too much planning raised too many doubts. You did what you could.

She ran down the list of crew members mentally: herself, Billie, and Wilks. Adcox and the other marines: Falk. Dunston. Tully, Leslie's hacker friend. And Jones . . .

They *were* a good group. The trial run had been successful; of course, it would be different in real time, but the crew seemed committed and confident enough to get past any trouble. The only part that worried her was getting past the guard ships—but they were watching for incoming transport mostly, had been posted to ward off a possibly infected ship or one manned by somebody dangerous, like the mad General Spears who had brought Billie and Wilks along as stowaways.

It should work. Ripley hoped it would be as

easy as it looked, but she knew from experience that things rarely were as easy as they looked.

She had concentrated so completely on getting the thing together that there hadn't been time to relax. Not that there had ever been time for that once she'd run into the aliens. For her, it hadn't been that long. In realtime, it had been the better part of a century. Now the fucking things owned Earth, and humankind was a third-class local power.

Her hatred for the creatures was as much a part of her as her hair color or height. It affected everything she did, was the force behind all she had gone through to get where she was. She smiled wryly. Where was she? Sitting in the dark preparing to lead a group of fighters to steal a ship, fly across the galaxy, capture the queen of queens. And, eventually, use their captive to lure and kill every one of the goddamned aliens.

Ripley sighed. The choices she had made were simple ones, of basic morality, right and wrong. But now it had gone beyond just her. This could cost lives, could mean the end of her own. She usually knew better than to try and take responsibility for the people around her, but this felt different.

Shit, it *always* felt different.

It helped to know one thing—she didn't want to die, but if it meant taking that queen bitch out, or taking the bitch's spawn, she would. That choice had been made after the *Nostromo*, and it had become everything to her. The things had cost her too much. Her crew. Her family. Her whole life. She had nothing else left.

Ripley closed her eyes and waited for the others.

9

Dunston and Tully walked down the corridor toward the entry of dock D6, loudly discussing station politics. When they turned the corner to the dock, they would be in a position to see any guard who might be present.

Dunston signaled to Ripley, Wilks, and Falk, who were following. No guard.

Wilks was close enough to see Tully pull a small keyboard from her pack and plug it into a panel set in the wall. She crouched down and quickly began to punch in codes.

"I don't know. I mean, it's one thing to *say* you're going to upgrade the conditions, but they've been saying that since I got here...."

Wilks and the others continued slowly toward the door while Tully checked for monitors.

Dunston droned on about the quality of the food served in the dining halls.

According to the deck layout in the computer, there wouldn't be any guard at this point. Ripley had insisted on a double check.

Tully looked up, grinning. "Clear," she said quietly.

Wilks felt himself loosen slightly. It was crucial to go unnoticed for as long as possible in order to get past the guard ships. Once an alarm was sounded, their chances fell damn fast.

The *Kurtz* was docked outside D6; to get to it they needed to open three doors—this one, the entry to the air lock, and the ship itself. All were computer-coded, and the complexity of the entry systems usually meant no human guards, a major selling point for their choice of transport.

They would get into the loading room and call in the rest of the crew; Captain McQuade's voice-print would be the key to the *Kurtz*. A licensed military pilot and the proper codes were all they needed to get on board. The codes Leslie and Tully had rascaled up with little trouble.

Maybe too little . . .

While Tully set up her portable, Wilks moved to the nearest 'com to raise Billie and the others. They were waiting in Brewster's quarters. The marines had taken all of the carbines and grenades from the armory they could carry, signing them out with General Peters's personal access code. Wilks had laughed when Leslie had suggested using the general's code.

Looked like Peters had helped out after all.

Wilks walked quickly down D-corridor to a public 'com and tapped in Brewster's number.

"Yeah?"

"Hey, Brewster, it's Wilks. Why don't you pop on over and have a drink?"

"Sounds great. Meet you at the bar."

Wilks discommed and walked back down the empty hall. So far, so good. Billie and the marines would be there in two minutes or less, barring complications, and then they would be on their way—

"Hey," came a voice from behind him.

Wilks stopped and turned around. A burly young man in a security uniform approached him slowly, face grim. His hand rested lightly on the butt of his stunner.

"Where do you think *you're* going?"

Brewster nodded at the other marines and they stood, picking up assorted wrapped bundles. Weapons, ammo, various tools. No one spoke. Billie went to help Jones with his equipment, a few bags of med supplies and a small diagnostic unit. He smiled at her, teeth bright against his chocolate-colored skin.

"Guess we're about to be outlaws," he said. He looked nervous.

Billie returned his smile. "You get used to it after a while," she said. "Besides, you already *are* an outlaw. Conspiracy."

Adcox went first, as scout. She carried nothing, and would walk a half a minute ahead of the others.

Brewster and McQuade went next.

Billie counted silently to ten.

Carvey and Moto stepped out.

Finally, Billie and Jones walked to the door.

Billie's heart pounded and she felt a tiny trickle of sweat run between her breasts in spite of the cool air.

Amy, she thought. They stepped out into the corridor.

Wilks smiled at the guard. "I'm trying to find a biolab, D2—isn't it down here?"

The guard seemed to relax slightly, but didn't smile back. "Wrong direction. The labs are back that way," he said, pointing behind them, "and go left at the first tee."

Wilks shook his head, still smiling. "Thanks."

The guard nodded and stepped past him, headed toward D6. Where the others would be waiting for Wilks.

"Are you sure it's not to the right?" said Wilks loudly, when he had gotten but a few paces away.

"Yeah, I'm sure. Now—"

"Because I went left before, I think, and I think it's right. I mean, headed back to the lifts is right, right?" He spoke in what he hoped was a stupid but friendly tone. And he hoped the others would hear him.

The guard turned and moved closer to Wilks, as if proximity would somehow make his answer plainer.

"Look. Go back. When you get to the tee, go left. *Left*. Got it?"

"Left. Uh-huh. Got it."

The guard shook his head. And distracted by Wilks's stupidity, just as Wilks had hoped he'd be, he walked away from D6.

Which was good, since otherwise Wilks would've had to take him out.

Wilks let out a breath and waited for a few seconds before heading back. They were grouped in front of the door, all except for Falk; the large man stepped out from behind a turn farther down the hall, obviously prepared to deal with any interruptions. They had heard him working the guard.

Tully had her finger on the entry button and was waiting for the go.

Ripley arched an eyebrow at Wilks.

"Let's do it," he said.

But before Tully could move, the door slid open.

A man in a worker's coverall stood there, holding what looked like a weapon.

Billie and Jones walked down the hall side by side, not speaking. They came to the first turn, and Billie caught a glimpse of Moto and Carvey as they turned the corner ahead. She relaxed slightly. Everything seemed to be working as planned, so far. She wondered how Ripley's team was doing.

Dunston stepped forward as if to greet the surprised worker. The mechanical device apparently wasn't a weapon; the man dropped it and raised clenched hands, mouth set. He was surprised, but obviously combative. They weren't supposed to be here and he knew it.

Dunston reached out, holding his hands so the backs of his wrists faced the worker. Ripley saw the man blink, confused—

The martial arts teacher moved forward quickly on his right foot, almost crouching. He flicked his fingers at the man's eyes.

The worker raised his arms to cover his face, and—

Dunston dropped flat onto the deck, did something fast with his legs—

The worker squawked once, fell, hit the deck, hard.

Wilks dropped and clapped a hand over the man's mouth, but the guy wasn't moving. Apparently he'd hit his head and was out cold.

It all happened in the space of a few breaths.

"Nice move," Wilks said.

"No one else inside now," Dunston said. "But hurry. Somebody's coming."

Billie and the doctor were almost to the dock when they heard footsteps running toward them.

Billie froze, laying her free hand on the doctor's arm. He stopped and looked at her, his own dark features a mask of anxiety. She felt as though time had slowed to a crawl, but excuses ran through her head at lightning speed. *We're on our way to a medical emergency, I'm assisting, he's a doctor, we're teaching a class—*

Adcox appeared in front of them, out of breath. Billie and Jones let out shuddery sighs in unison, but the lieutenant's expression was frantic. She grabbed one of their bags.

"Trouble," she said, and turned back toward the dock.

Billie fell in beside Char and Jones at a jog. Adcox hadn't wasted any more air by telling them what had happened, and Billie didn't ask; they would find out soon enough.

Wilks dragged the worker inside before turning to Dunston. "Who's coming?" he said.

"Another worker."

"How—?" Wilks started to ask Dunston how he could possibly know, if he'd had some extrasensory flash or something, when he saw the evidence himself.

There was a table in one corner of the large room where the downed man had evidently been about to sit for breakfast. Except that there were two trays set out, two chairs, and two steaming cups of dark liquid.

"Pretty mystical," said Dunston. "Ancient secret of the Orient, multiple-coffee awareness."

Adcox arrived, trailed by Billie and Jones.

Wilks turned to her. "Get everyone in here, now. We're expecting company."

Tully was already working on the air lock; Falk had stepped back into the corridor to help the others bring in the equipment.

Wilks looked at Ripley and saw the same question on her face that he felt on his own: How much time?

•   •   •

Billie ran into the workroom, Falk shut the door behind her, and Carvey crouched to the floor with a welder. Light too bright to look at flashed. Carvey quickly melted part of the heavy plastic door to the frame and then stepped back.

Moto unpacked one of the carbines and pointed it at the now-jammed entry.

Tully tapped in codes at the air lock.

"Come *on*," said Ripley, jaw tight.

"Okay, okay . . ." said Tully, almost to herself. "And—got it!"

The air lock door slid open. Tully unplugged her portable and ran the few steps to the hatch of the *Kurtz*. She hooked the portable to the new hatch.

McQuade stepped in after her. The others stood tensed, ready to rush in—

Behind them, the door mechanism to the D6 entry buzzed. It buzzed again, longer this time, the sound edged with a high-pitched mechanical whine. It could have only been a second or two, but it seemed a lot longer. Then someone pounded at the door.

"Diestler!" called a female voice, muffled through the thick plastic. "Hey, open up!"

The man on the floor groaned slightly and rolled his head to one side. Diestler, apparently.

Moto pointed her weapon at him, but he didn't move again.

Ripley turned to look at Wilks, but he was already headed to the entryway.

The pounding continued. "You asshole! This shit's getting cold, open *up!*"

Wilks punched the entry button. The mechanism whined again, but the door remained closed.

"Hold on!" shouted Wilks. "Door's stuck!"

There was a pause. Ripley gritted her teeth and hoped that Wilks sounded at least remotely like the unconscious worker.

"Well, no shit," said the woman on the other side. "Come on, wonder-tech, fix the goddamn thing, my breakfast is dying out here."

Ripley could see the crew members relax a little. Wilks had just bought them a little time.

Tully stopped typing and motioned for McQuade to step forward. A quiet computerized voice came from the monitor at face level.

"Command pilot please enter vocal access code now."

"McQuade, Eric D., captain. A-seven-zero-five-oh-B," he said.

"Thank you."

Tully input the final code, a grin spreading across her face. With a triumphant flourish, she pressed "enter."

Ripley grinned. Almost there—

Nothing happened.

"Invalid code. Access denied. Please enter new code now."

Wilks picked up the tool that Diestler had dropped and stared at it. It was some kind of computer hookup, an oblong box with several conductors and prongs on one side.

The woman called impatiently from the other side. "Come on, Diestler, or I'm going to sit on the fucking floor and eat it all—yours, too. Don't tell me you did this door all by yourself while I was gone."

Wilks looked at the box in his hands and stopped. Of course, of *course*!

"Diestler? Say something." The woman sounded suspicious now. "What are you doing, anyway? You beating off in there or something?"

"Just a sec," said Wilks. "I'm trying the code on this one." It would have to hold her. He turned and ran, as quietly as he could, back to the air lock.

"I don't *have* any new codes!" said Tully. "This is it! They must have changed them since yesterday!"

The crew stood around her, tense.

"Can we blow the door?" said Jones.

"Not without alarms," said Falk. The big man looked angry. "And that wouldn't do us much good, to have a big fucking *hole* in our escape ship."

Billie felt despair rise inside her. To be stopped by a fucking *door*—

Wilks shoved past her and handed a box to Tully. "Plug this in," he said. "Quick!"

She grabbed it and jammed the conductor into the opening of her portable.

Ripley looked at Wilks. "What—"

"New access codes, got to be. The general is more paranoid than we thought."

The hatch of the *Kurtz* popped open.

● ● ●

McQuade and Ripley strapped themselves in at the console while the others moved around behind them, preparing for flight. Wilks stood next to the two pilots. With any luck, the female tech hadn't alerted anyone yet. If she had, they would be thoroughly fucked.

As McQuade punched the disengage controls, a voice crackled out over the intercom.

"Ah, *Kurtz* pilot, identify yourself, please."

"This is Captain Eric McQuade. And who is this?" He spoke gruffly, impatiently.

"Sir. This is Lieutenant Dunn, sir, of the *Kirkland*. Please state purpose and authorization. Sir."

"Operation Arrowhead," said McQuade. He sounded bored. "Access P-two-one-four-oh-two." General Peters's code.

There was a pause. "Sir? We have no missions scheduled from this sector." Dunn sounded very young and very nervous. "Could you please wait while I raise the general—sir?"

"Jesus Christ! Peters schedules another bughunt without telling some dumbshit lieutenant and now we have to wait until you drag him out of bed to okay it *again*? Think, son! Why would we want to go on this trip? For *fun*?" McQuade paused. "Fine. Go ahead. But you better hope the general is in a good mood. Lieutenant."

There was another pause, and Dunn spoke again, obviously cowed. "I'm sorry, sir. Um. Go ahead, access cleared and verified. Good luck, sir."

Wilks and Ripley grinned at one another and Wilks slapped McQuade on the back. From behind them, Wilks could hear the others laughing. He walked back to strap himself in, feeling vaguely sorry for Lieutenant Dunn; by the time he got hold of the general for verification, they'd be way out of range. And there would be hell to pay for it. Too bad.

Billie smiled at him when he sat down. "Score one for the good guys," she said.

He adjusted his seat before he answered. "That was the easy part."

She nodded, and her smile faltered slightly. Wilks leaned his head against the back of his chair and let out a deep breath.

They were in it all the way now.

10

Ripley was the last one awake on the *Kurtz*. She double-checked the course setting in the dimly lit room, shivering slightly from the cold. She wore only a tank top and underwear, fine for the sleep chamber but little protection from the frigid stillness of the ship; the air warmers and recyclers had already been dialed down to minimum. The system would kick back on a couple of hours before they woke up—or before *she* woke up. She had reset the controls on her chamber to rouse her an hour before the others. No good reason, really, just instinct.

The last of the preparations made, she turned away from the computer and padded barefoot to her chamber. All around her, the crew members rested, already in their own dreamworlds. Ripley hoped they slept well; so far, the men and women of the *Kurtz* had done okay, and she was glad to have their help.

She looked around the room a final time before climbing into her own sleep-box, and wondered if she would dream during the sleep that was so like a shadow of death. . . .

Ripley shivered again as she triggered the mechanism, but not so much from the cold as before.

Wilks had been here before, he was sure of it. He was standing in a dark place, the air around him alive with fear and tension.

"—they're all around us!" Someone yelled behind him. Familiar, like the rest of it. A warning horn screamed somewhere ahead of him in the hot, wet darkness. Huge coils of glistening black covered the walls all around him.

"No," he said softly.

It couldn't be. He, they were on Rim. Where the aliens had killed his unit, where he was going to die—

"Shut the fuck up!" Wilks yelled out. He knew what had to be done. He'd done it before. "Maintain your field of fire, we're gonna be fine!"

Eight of the squad were dead; as a corporal, he was ranking noncom, he had to stay in control—

He heard shots in the alien den; the sound of a caseless carbine pounded his ears.

A little girl clung to his arm, crying. Billie.

"Easy, honey," he said. As he picked her up she turned her tear-streaked face up to look at him while all around the creatures screamed and weapons screamed back at them. "We're gonna be fine. We're going back to the ship, everything is gonna be okay."

He was trying to run but his legs had been dipped in plastecrete. Everything was happening too fast and he couldn't *move*. He shouted more orders, unable to see who he called out to. Who was left?

"Shoot for targets, triplets only! We don't have enough ammo to waste on full auto suppressive fire!"

There was a sealed door ahead. They would have to cut their way out, fast. The reactor was approaching meltdown and a swarm of the killing things was right behind—

Billie screamed when he tried to put her down. God, she was so small, so helpless! "I gotta open the door," he said.

Someone stepped out of the darkness to hold her. He turned, grateful, and—

"Leslie?" She was dressed in camo, a carbine slung over one shoulder.

"Got her," she said. She smiled easily.

Wrong, this part was wrong—

No time to think. He pulled a plasma cutter from his belt, triggered it. The stacked carbon lock melted and ran like water as he waved the cutter back and forth.

The door slid up.

He knew what was coming, knew that the queen would be there, waiting to take him. He had dreamed it before. . . .

But—no.

He stepped forward into a black, empty corridor and the sounds behind him fell away. It was dead quiet.

Billie stood there. Not the little girl she had been only a minute before. She was grown, a woman, wearing an untabbed soldier's uniform. He could see one of her small breasts exposed, glistening with sweat. She walked toward him, her face calm and beautiful.

"David," she whispered, and pressed up against him.

His lower belly tingled, penis suddenly hard and straining.

He felt dizzy. No, this was wrong. But he went with it. "Billie," he said, "we have to get out of here, there's no time—"

She silenced his mouth with hers, traced his lips with her soft tongue. He closed his eyes as she moved her hands over his chest and downward, circling. . . .

As he gave himself over to the pleasure, the noise behind them suddenly washed back over him. Alarms and gunfire and screams—

He jerked himself away from Billie and grabbed at his belt, opening his eyes. Quickly, a weapon, something—!

He was alone, unarmed. He spun around in a circle, looking for Billie, looking for anybody—

He heard the aliens getting closer, but couldn't see anything.

A computer-chip voice informed him that meltdown would occur in five seconds.

"No!" he cried out, fell to his knees. "No, no, no—"

"Three seconds. Two. One. Meltdown—"

The world turned white.

Billie and Ripley walked side by side down a dark, debris-littered tunnel on Earth. It was neither warm nor cold; the air was still and silent. Billie turned to look at Ripley several times, but the older woman kept her eyes straight ahead.

They were looking for Amy. Billie guessed that they were in some kind of transportation shaft; she wanted to ask Ripley, but couldn't find the words. She said nothing.

Billie felt anxious, scared that they would miss Amy somehow. She was reassured that Ripley was with her, knew that if anyone could find the little girl, it would be her. Besides, it didn't matter who found her, as long as she was okay. . . .

They came to a fork in the tunnel, both of the corridors leading off into darkness. Without speaking, Ripley started down the one to the left. Billie wanted to go with her, but Amy could be in either one. She walked into the other tunnel alone.

She kept up a steady pace for what seemed like hours, headed in a straight line. The only sounds were her footsteps and breathing, echoing off into nothing. She knew she shouldn't be able to see at all, there being no lights, but for some reason she could make out each section of the tunnel for a few feet in front of her. She walked on.

Suddenly, she heard a sound ahead of her. She

stopped and listened. A child was crying, the lonely wail carrying through the dark corridor and surrounding her. The acoustics were distorted; she couldn't tell how far away she was. . . .

"Amy!" She called out.

The crying continued.

Billie started to run, certain that it was her. "Hold on, Amy! I'm coming!" The sound of her voice was strange and somehow flat in the echoey chamber.

She ran for a long time until she saw a bend in the tunnel. She knew that Amy would be around the corner, and cried out, happy. After all this time, finally—

"Amy!" She ran around the corner. Stopped, heart pounding. Dark despair fell onto her, a hard rain, cold and awful.

The tunnel forked again into five spokes. Far away she could hear Amy crying, and try as she might she couldn't tell which tunnel it came from.

"Where *are* you?" She called out, but there was no answer except for the sobs of the lost little girl.

Billie sank to the floor, feeling more alone than she ever had in her life, cradling her head in her arms. She began to cry herself, feeling as lost and scared as the unseen child.

From somewhere distant, she heard someone call her name, but it wasn't Amy. She didn't have the strength to reply, and she didn't care. She would never find Amy, she knew that now.

She wept until she was awash in tears. There was no hope.

No hope at all.

11

Ripley slipped her feet into a pair of boots and yawned widely. She felt grainy and exhausted, hung over from sleep. She knew that it would eventually wear off once she got moving, but that didn't stop her from a vague, wistful feeling as she looked around at the slumbering crew members. There were times when just staying asleep seemed infinitely better than getting up.

She sighed, stood, stretched her arms over her head, then bent to touch her toes. A half-remembered line occurred to her as she flexed her arms—something about an early bird getting the jump on others. The air cyclers had kicked on as scheduled, a low mechanical hum in the quiet sleep area, but the room was still cold enough for her breath to show. It would be warmer by the time the others got up—apparently early birds were hot-blooded creatures.

Her sleep had been deep and dreamless and she had awakened, though not refreshed, at least ready to get on with things. Her general plan to get the queen to Earth was okay, if perhaps not altogether reasonable. The specifics were still hazy. Like getting the goddamned thing onboard, for one—the creature probably wasn't going to just hop into the hold if they asked politely: *Excuse me, bitch, would you step this way?*

Well, one thing at a time; they had three days before they reached the queen's planet, plenty of time to come up with something.

Ripley had seen the layout of the *Kurtz* onscreen back at Gateway, but maybe walking it would trigger some ideas.

She went out into the chilled corridor.

The *Kurtz* was a two-function freighter, built not only for deepspace but also to enter a planet's gravity and land. It was shaped like an old-style bullet with fins—flat on the bottom, with rudimentary wings—and was aerodynamic, more or less. She'd learned to fly in similar vessels, had gotten her ticket as a pilot in a ship not too different from this one.

The upper level where she now stood was a series of rooms bisected by a main corridor that ran the length of the vessel. The command control room was forward and to her left. Across from her were a series of doors running down the hall: crew's quarters.

So, let's take a little tour, shall we?

She began to walk to the rear of the ship.

Each room would have its own 'fresher, but the shower was communal to help regulate water supply. It stood in between the last cubicle and a small workout room. Beyond the gym and aft was the med center, which looked cold and sterile behind the clear plexiflex door. With any luck, they'd have no need for the facility. . . .

She reached the corridor's end, then turned back toward the front. To her left now was a large supply area where the marines had stored their equipment before hitting the sleep chambers. Past that, the mess. Ripley's stomach growled noisily at the thought of food. She stopped and looked in at the bolted-down tables and chairs. It would also serve as a conference room. She reluctantly walked on, deciding to wait and eat with the others.

Adjacent to the eating area she was back where she started, at the sleep chambers. All in all, a good enough ship. It was a bit larger than they really needed, but that wasn't a handicap; besides, she reminded herself, thieves can't always be choosy.

She shook her head. She was in trouble again, win or lose.

She walked into the command area and past the twenty-plus seats for crew takeoffs and landings, into the partitioned-off pilot's room. She stood for a moment and watched the console, its colored lights blinking or glowing in the dim chamber. No problems, of course. An alarm would have gone off. She stepped away from the board and to one of the ship's five stairwells, to check out the lower deck.

Ripley walked through the computer room and the APC bay without really looking. She felt her heart speed up a bit as she came to a stop in front of the double hatch to the cargo area. This was what she had wanted to see, the queen's new home. She took a deep breath of the frigid air and stepped inside.

It was a huge chamber, coated heavily with carbslip on every exposed surface except the work lights; those were behind thick plates of kleersteel. The acid-resistant gray coating of the carbslip made the chamber seem like what she imagined a giant intestine might look like from the inside. The coating was dry, but it had a greasy, almost slimy shine to it. There were two stairwells, leading to the sleep chambers and mess, respectively. Both sets of stairs ended at airtight and extra-thick pressure doors. They would want to reinforce those before admitting their cargo, just to be sure. This place would safely hold the most noxious biochemical and radioactive wastes men could produce. The engineers who designed the hold knew the vile cargo would normally be glass-crated solids or liquid in insulated barrels, but in a pinch, the doors could be sealed and the stuff pumped in through special piping so the whole chamber could be turned into something like a giant toxic aquarium.

The only sound in the room was her own breathing. She looked around the chamber and nodded slowly: a suitable place for the bitch queen. Let her dull her teeth and claws on the impervious carbslip; let her sit like a bug in a jar, wondering what her fate was to be. Fuck her.

She had seen what she'd needed to, and the crew would be waking shortly. What she really needed was something to eat and a hot shower. She'd had no startling revelations, but perhaps one of the others had dreamed something up—

She started back to the open stairs in the computer room. Maybe their closer proximity to the planet would offer more detailed dreams, ideas that they could use. It was just a thought—but then, their mission wasn't exactly based on solid facts so far, she thought as the thick treadplate steps rang hollowly under her boots.

She grinned to herself as she moved through the slowly warming rooms, back toward the sleep chambers. Maybe the queen *would* tell them how to trap her if they asked politely. It wouldn't be much crazier than the rest of this trip.

Wilks heard a few muttered groans from the other crew members as they climbed from their sleep chambers and stretched, put on clothes, came back to life. He swiveled his head and tried to relieve the tightness deep between his shoulder blades. He'd had worse hangovers, but coming out of cold sleep always left him feeling disoriented and spacey. He'd dreamed, although he couldn't quite remember—

"Good morning, Wilks." Billie.

She walked over to stand by him, clenched and

unclenched her fingers slowly. She looked pale. "You seen Ripley?"

Part of his dream came back to him when he looked at her, more of a feeling than a picture. Something sexual about Billie. He turned away from her slightly, uncomfortable.

"No. I hope she's making coffee, though." He hoped he sounded more at ease than he felt.

She nodded and walked toward the showers.

Wilks tabbed his boots. Maybe he'd shower after breakfast.

He yawned. Then he followed several of the others down the corridor and into the mess.

Ripley had indeed made coffee, in addition to putting out several trays of food packets and utensils. She sat at one of the long cafeteria tables, poking at her plate of steaming gray muck.

Wilks poured a cup of coffee and grabbed a tray with a foil pouch labeled "stir-fry." He sat down across from Ripley.

"Hey, Ripley. You're up early."

She nodded and watched him pour the contents of his activated packet onto his tray. It smelled like stir-fry, but was the same mottled soypro-gray as Ripley's. He grimaced.

"You'd think they'd invest in some food coloring," she said. "Sleep okay?"

"As well as could be expected. It's the getting out of bed that's a bitch."

She nodded again and went back to eating. Respectful of her silence, Wilks turned and focused his attention on the other crew members who straggled in.

McQuade looked haggard and irritable, and Brewster started in on him.

"Buddha, Cap, you look like shit."

Brewster turned to Carvey. "You know, they say it's harder for the old to travel like this."

McQuade fixed Brewster with a cold stare. "Yeah, well, it would have helped if I could have slept better. The sound of you virgins jacking off the whole time next to me kept me awake."

Carvey snickered.

Brewster tried to think of a comeback and came up short. He stalled, said, "Aw, gee, sorry about that, Cap, I—"

McQuade cut him off. "Yeah, well, your mother's sorry, too. At least that's what she told me when her mouth wasn't full in my quarters back on Gateway."

Even Brewster laughed at this.

Wilks smiled. The corporal was outmatched.

Moto and Falk walked in together and picked up trays.

"What's this?" said Falk. He pointed at a plate of crumbly tan substance.

"Ah, the famed and much-loved military instant corn bread," said Moto, putting a piece on her tray. "You get used to it."

"Like Brewster's mother," said Adcox. She smiled sweetly at Brewster.

He stabbed a chunk of soypro off his plate. "Oh, funny, Adcox."

Wilks was amused by the banter but felt a pang of bitter nostalgia listening to it. Talking the talk was an integral part of the military life; some things hadn't changed. It had been a long time since he had been in a group like this—he could almost hear his old friends talking, their voices superimposed over the *Kurtz*'s crew's. Jasper, Cassady, Ellis, Quinn, Lewis—and as always, he felt the guilt. He was still alive and they were dead.

Billie walked in and pulled her damp hair into a ponytail as she considered the food choices.

Wilks started to call her over when Adcox motioned for her to join her group. Billie waved at Wilks and Ripley as she sat down and started chatting with the other three.

Wilks sipped his coffee and noticed that both of the male soldiers perked up considerably when Billie sat down, Brewster in particular. He grinned at her as Carvey recounted some story involving a trip to a bar on Gateway.

Wilks was surprised by a sudden feeling of protectiveness toward Billie. Brewster wasn't her type, he was sure. She needed someone more mature, she had been through a lot, she needed somebody who could appreciate that—

Like me, he thought uneasily.

Ridiculous. They'd had opportunities before and decided to let them go by. What he felt for Billie was friendship, shared experiences.

But that dream—

Wilks looked away from Billie's group. Good that she had found some people her own age to hang around, finally. And maybe he was just developing some paternal instincts for her. . . .

Yeah. Right.

•   •   •

Billie found that she liked Dylan Brewster a lot. He was self-effacing in a mildly sarcastic way, had a bright smile, was very amiable. He and Tom Carvey played off of each other well; their affection for each other was obvious—and in spite of herself, she hoped that it was only brotherly.

She made herself think of Mitch as she listened to them talk, poking at an old wound that suddenly seemed important to feel. Yes, she still missed him, still hurt thinking of him. Ought not to be sitting here thinking about another man.

Jesus, she was having *breakfast* with him, not screwing him. And yet each time Brewster turned his eyes her way she felt a slight tingle in the pit of her stomach.

Billie looked over at Wilks, who stared moodily into his coffee. What was she to him, exactly? Or he to her? She felt bonded to him somehow, some kind of—

Too much to think about. She felt tired already, worrying about relationships not an hour out of sleep. Troubled sleep at that. She had looked for Amy, running through her dreams and never finding her. Amy, she reminded herself, was the important thing.

Ripley stood up and looked around the room. "Excuse me," she said. "Everyone is here, so I'd like to throw out a suggestion."

The room quieted. Billie laid down her fork.

"Thanks. I'm thinking that our dreams might tell us something new this close to the planet," she said. "Maybe a more exact location, maybe numbers of aliens, something. I'd like you all to see if you can remember what you dream tonight, so tomorrow we can talk about it.

"One thing that all of your files showed is that you're highly creative and sensitive people. Spend some time thinking about it. I'm open to ideas, so if you think of anything, let me know."

She sat down again and started talking quietly with Wilks.

"Think of anything like *what*?" said Carvey.

"Do you understand 'idea,' Carv? It's kind of like a thought, but it's newer." Brewster smiled, pleased with himself.

"You wipe. I understand that you're as 'sensitive' as my skivvies—"

Billie tuned out the soldiers' talk and thought about what Ripley had said. She dreaded the dreams, had tried all sorts of meds back on Gateway to avoid them—and now they were going to be stronger, more detailed. She shuddered slightly at the thought. Her earliest memories were of bad dreams. She'd never been able to keep them at bay for long, either. Damn.

Then again, she told herself as she looked around at the pallid faces of the crew, there were worse things than dreams. They'd all found that out; humanity as a whole knew it all too well.

Brewster gave her a smile and she returned it, noting the slight flush in his cheeks. Well. At least she wasn't alone anymore. They were all in this together.

12

Keith Dunston stood in the black lair of the queen. The air was moist and hot; somewhere water dripped and somewhere else it flowed. He was surrounded by soft clicking and chittering, like fingernails tapping upon glass, or impossible creatures rustling in the dark. He knew which it was, and he also knew it was a dream.

He held his hands up in front of his face and counted his fingers. He breathed slowly and evenly; the trick was one he had used before, and in his subconscious wanderings it had always placed him in control. Of course, this was different; this was not of his own mind. But command of the transmission was not necessary, merely command of *himself*.

A huge shadow shifted in front of him, moved closer.

He could just make out her shape—taller than the Earth breed, longer, more powerful and sturdy.

Come to me—

The voice in his mind was inflected with great love and longing. His brain translated her need into something he would understand, would know, had known before.

He closed his eyes and concentrated on a response as he had done before, always to no avail. Perhaps this time—

Where are you? I must find you.

Come to me, I love you, I am waiting—

Yes. Are there others?

Dunston waited, eyes closed. The sounds of the alien breed moving intensified, filled the air. All around him now, they moved closer. Her children. Hundreds, perhaps thousands answered his questions only with their shifting, sliding, greasy motions, making noises like some insane hybrid of locust and wild plains animal.

The dream was different from before, more vivid. He sensed the texture of the nest's floor beneath his feet, felt the heat emanating from the alien construct around him. The smell was overwhelming, rot and decay and vomit and a bathroom with a bad chemical recycler. Even so, the emotional impact of the queen's desire was far greater; it would overwhelm him were he to open himself to it. The mother's love enshrouded him, tried to enter him with all the subtlety of a rapist.

Dunston raised his hands in front of his chest and placed his palms together, index fingers extended. The first of the nine kanji, of Kuji Kiri; Tu Mo, the channel of control . . .

The queen beckoned, a repeated cycle of need as Dunston calmed his heart and mind with the simple gestures. Stillness, now. Motion, action—those would come later.

In the dreams, there was time to be still.

Falk was in the hot, stuffy shithole where *she* and her offspring dwelled. The fucking queen. He had been here before, but this time was different somehow. It looked the same, what he could see of it, but it was—*more*. The air was dank, sweaty, warm glue against his face. It was all alive, the place, the weird moving noises—like he was standing in the belly of some huge beast.

He waited, full of anger and dread, for her to speak.

Come to me—

The hulking darkness in front of him moved, started forward. He raised his arms, hands clenched, and waited for her to come closer. He wanted to destroy, to rip her fucking head off and dance on her bones. Her children had taken Marla away—

Falk felt sadness splash over him, felt it engulf him in its flow like a dark and lonely tide. These brainless, giant fucking insects had ripped his life apart, had made the universe smaller and colder. Why Marla? Why?

I understand—

The voice in his head was simple and calm, full of strength. Not the queen, not the whispery, strange androgynous sound of the queen ... He lowered his hands, suddenly unsure.

"Marla?" he said. His voice was thick and quavering, swallowed in the muggy air. It was impossible.

I love you.

It *was* her voice, the lilt of it familiar and emotional, with that husky undertone he thought he'd never hear again.

He tried to step forward, but his feet wouldn't move. He looked around wildly, but he couldn't see in the murky darkness. Couldn't see if maybe Marla had somehow made it to this hellish place.

Come to me, I'm waiting—

Falk suddenly realized that he wasn't hearing the words aloud, that they were in his mind only. And that his mind was where Marla existed, and nowhere else. The message was the queen's; it was a trick. For one minute he had actually hoped—

His grief and confusion dissipated, were replaced by a searing anger so great that his whole body shook. Everything was tinted red; the blackness rippled and flowed with the new heat of the color.

Falk drew in breath to scream, to cry, to vent his fury and seal the queen's fate, and all of it disappeared and went gray. . . .

Charlene Adcox stood in the queen's steamy chamber and tried to damp down her fear. She was scared, but being scared, she admonished herself, shouldn't stop one from getting things done. Her own mother had told her that many times, and she believed it still. Although her psych visits with Dr. Torchin had helped her see that she suppressed her emotions, was cut off from her feelings. . . .

It wasn't important now. She took in her surroundings, careful to let no detail slip by.

The place she was in was like a sauna, but the heat was wet and foul, the warmth of rot. It was dark, the only light coming from a few cracks in the roof of the nest, far above. There were sounds of water and movement around her, but it was centered . . . behind and to the left, and again beyond her, past where the darkness was thicker.

I need you, I love you—

The queen moved forward, her words echoing in Adcox's mind. With it, as before, came hints of other things, information that was not human. Tangential reference points, telemetry data, star charts seen with tunneled vision and delivered with the strength of utter supremacy. And purpose. It was all much clearer now—

Adcox could feel the emotional force that the queen radiated, but was not pulled by it. The love was huge but impersonal; her own thoughts were stronger, controllable in the chaos of feelings.

I wait for you—

When the queen spoke, Adcox got a sense of where she was, a curving roundness in water. The design was alien, complex but organic, somewhere . . .

The lieutenant concentrated, tried to force the image into geographical planes, but it wouldn't come. The beckoning was meant for different instincts than she could claim, terrifying in its insane pattern.

Suddenly the queen stepped even closer, close enough for Adcox to reach out and touch. Her attempts to put aside her fear vanished.

This isn't supposed to happen—!

Adcox screamed, any illusion of control gone, as the queen lifted a wormy, clawed arm to stroke her. . . .

13

Billie sat in the dining hall next to Char and sipped black coffee. She watched as the others filed in; they all looked like she felt. Dark circles beneath the eyes, pale faces, wired on nervous tension.

She had awakened frightened and angry from the queen's message, amazed at how much more real it had been. She had learned nothing new, except that the planet they would reach the next day was the right one. It had to be—the difference in dream intensity was staggering.

Billie hadn't slept after her dream, and she'd heard Char scream sometime after dawn; their quarters were side by side. She glanced at her friend, worried, but the lieutenant seemed to be holding up. They had sat up together until it was

113

time for the meeting, talking about anything but the dreams.

Wilks was the last to arrive. He looked like he had slept okay; Billie felt a mild surge of envy when she remembered that he wasn't one of the dreamers.

Ripley leaned against one of the tables, arms folded. After Wilks sat, she began to speak.

"Good morning. I can tell nobody slept well, and we all know why. Now I'd like to hear if any of you got anything new from it."

"Well, it's the right planet," said Billie. Everyone else nodded.

"Fuckin' A," said Carvey.

"Good to know," said Ripley. "Adcox—you were the only one who saw *where* before . . ."

"She's got her nest set up in a lake or a swamp," Char said. Her voice was unemotional, dead. "I couldn't tell you where exactly. Someplace warm, obviously. It's rounded, like a dome—at least part of it is. And she's much stronger than the Earth breed."

Dunston nodded. "More powerful in body and intellect," he said. "And she's got an entire legion with her. Hundreds."

Ripley sighed. "Yeah, I was afraid of that. Anyone else get a fix on location?"

Dr. Jones cleared his throat. "She's at the hottest part of the planet. I didn't see the shape of it, but it *is* in some body of shallow water and it's wherever the temperature is most consistently warm."

"Good," said Ripley. "That's good. What else?"

It was quiet. Billie looked around the room. Brewster caught her gaze for a moment and smiled tiredly at her. She wondered how he was doing. He and Carvey remained silent. Falk stared at his hands, expression unreadable. Moto and Tully also looked around and waited for someone to speak.

Wilks stood and broke the tension. "We're close enough to get a good read on planet type, maybe find the hot spots. Tully, you want to do some checking?"

The woman nodded and picked up her coffee cup.

"Okay," Ripley said. "I know it's been rough, but we're going to be there tomorrow and we still need to get ready for a few things. McQuade and I are going to work on some mechanical suits after breakfast and we could use help. Meet down in the loading dock in half an hour."

The meeting was over. Billie didn't feel particularly hungry, but she went to a food dispenser and scanned the selection anyway. Maybe eating would wake her up a little. She punched in some mad scientist's version of eggs and bread. Char followed her.

"So current crisis aside, what are we going to do when we get her to Earth?" Char said. "Anyone thought that far ahead?"

"I don't know. I guess we'll worry about it if we make it that far."

Char chewed at her lip but didn't say anything else.

The food arrived in little sealed biodegradable packages, hot, but ugly.

As Billie choked down her order of scrambled soypro, she thought about Char's question. What were they going to do? Knowing the answers hadn't been a major part of this whole business so far, had it?

Ripley was surprised by McQuade's query.

"Orona's bombs," she said. "Isn't it obvious? They were never set off."

McQuade shrugged. "I don't know about anybody named 'Orona.' "

They had started on the loader suits; the others would be down in a few minutes. They were taking apart the *Kurtz*'s two power loaders in an attempt to make four new ones. Smaller, lighter, less overall protection, but better armor than none. The sounds of their work echoed in the big chamber.

Ripley laid down her wrench and turned to McQuade. "Orona was a government scientist. He conceived a plan to detonate nuclear bombs in the infested areas. He got it set up but then died before they could be triggered."

"Why didn't somebody else do it?"

It was Ripley's turn to shrug. "Some malfunction, maybe. Maybe somebody got cold feet when it came time to push the button. Probably anybody who could say is dead."

McQuade snorted.

"Well, that's why we're here, Captain." She

picked up the wrench and started in on one of the loader's clamps.

"So how did you find out about Orona?" said McQuade.

Ripley unhooked the mechanical arm and set it on the floor. "Common knowledge, or so I thought."

"Yeah. It just seems that the corps would have access to that information, and I never heard of it. . . ."

Ripley gave him a tight grin. "That's the military for you. A group dedicated to making sure nobody gets to know what they know. They hoard little bits of trivia like diamonds and shit steel bricks if anyone finds out—when most people couldn't care less, much less use it for some diabolical purpose." She suddenly remembered who she was talking to. "No offense meant."

"None taken. I agree with you. The marine involvement in this crisis has been poorly organized from the start. Bunch of generals running around and flapping their arms and basically achieving zero. Why I'm here."

They went back to work, setting aside the pieces of machinery to be reassembled later. Ripley liked McQuade. He knew what he was doing and worked quickly and efficiently. At this rate, they'd be half done before anyone showed up. That McQuade didn't know about the bombs, though . . .

She tried to recall who had told her about Orona's plan and drew a blank. She had heard it sometime after the second LV-426 trip but before Gateway—

Brewster, Carvey, Adcox, and Billie arrived at the dock and headed toward them.

McQuade raised an eyebrow at Ripley.

"Go ahead," she said. "They *are* marines."

She watched as McQuade gave orders. Billie sat on the floor and sorted out different-sized holding pins and screws while the three soldiers set to work on cannibalizing the second loader. Power wrenches hummed, the smell of lube and reluctant-to-move metal hung in the air.

Funny, that McQuade had looked to her before he ordered the marines. She knew that the crew thought of her as the leader, but was vaguely surprised that it felt so ... natural.

She turned her mind back to the project and made a mental note to ask the others about Orona after lunch.

Wilks leaned over Tully's shoulder and scanned the readout on the planet.

"Atmosphere's breathable, but just barely," she said. "High in contaminants, low in oxygen."

"Could be worse," said Wilks. "Bulking around out there in a climate suit would be a bitch."

"Plenty of water. Almost eighty percent ocean and plenty of lakes—nasty, too. Full of trace elements and probably local bugs. Drinking it wouldn't do you any good."

Wilks leaned closer. Gravity was almost half a gee higher than Earth's; good thing their crew was a strong group physically. "Don't drink the water, don't breathe the air?"

"Huh?"

"Old joke. What else?" he said. "Weather, plants, animals—?"

"It's windy," said Tully, "at least in the mountainous regions. Landing should be a thrill. Vegetation must live on heat and poison, 'cause the sun don't shine much through the cloud cover. It won't be pretty. Got to be some animals, though I haven't seen any."

Wilks heard that. Fucking monsters had to eat something. It could be worse—but they were about to set down on a hot, wet, poisoned planet where jogging would be an effort for the strongest of them. To try and overpower the almighty-top-of-the-heap-queen-fucking-head alien on her own ground. Great.

Well, hey. No problem, the marines were lean, mean, and obscene.

Yeah. Right.

"Okay," he said. "See if you can pinpoint the warmest areas for the flyby tomorrow."

He leaned against the wall and watched Tully dig for the information. The mother queen had no doubt picked a charming spot to build her home, and she probably wouldn't want to move without a fight.

Another bad place to die. And as he had thought so many times before, it was probably going to happen this trip. The universe could only pass out so much luck to any one guy and he'd sure as shit gone through his share a long while ago.

Well. What the hell. If it was your turn, there wasn't anything you could do. If it wasn't, he guessed he would find out soon enough.

14

Billie stroked Dylan's hair and watched him sleep; his legs were warm and smooth against her own. She wasn't scared to go to sleep—her fear of the dream lessened with a partner in her bed. Interesting, that sex instilled such a sense of peace. She felt relaxed and calm, but just too introspective to doze off.

He murmured in his sleep and rolled away from her. Dylan Brewster. He had shown up at her door a few hours before and asked if she wanted company. She felt a tiny, delicious shiver run down her spine as she looked at him now, the way he had asked politely to stay the night. Quite the gentleman . . . at first, anyway. The sex had been passionate and wild.

Billie remembered having read somewhere that

sex was a normal reaction in threatening circumstances, a life-affirming instinct. That was probably so; she liked the young soldier a lot and was glad to have him there. But she was not in love with him—

She thought of Mitch and was surprised that it didn't hurt so much anymore. Whatever regrets she had over their short time together, it wasn't connected to having made love with Dylan. Mitch had only wanted her to feel loved and whole, whether or not he could be there; she doubted that he would begrudge her some peace of mind now.

In the morning, the crew would meet to discuss final plans for carrying out their mission. They would be dropping onto the planet in a little less than twelve hours. Her stomach tightened at the thought; if everything went perfectly, they could be on their way back to Earth soon afterward. She was nervous, but excited, too. It felt good to be on the offensive for a change, to fight actively instead of always running away. And maybe to make a difference for the people left on Earth . . .

Billie moved down beneath the cover, snuggling against her new lover for warmth. He turned toward her and opened his eyes halfway.

"Hey," he said, voice heavy with sleep. "You okay?"

"Yeah. Just thinking."

He yawned and closed his eyes, but smiled slightly.

"What about?" he said, and slid one hand between her legs. She parted them and leaned back.

"I thought you were out for the night," she said, and inhaled sharply as he slipped a finger into her.

"I am. Just ignore me," he said.

Billie laughed and touched his erection, moved her hand up and down the silky-textured skin. He moaned as she crawled over him, covering his body with hers. She felt him slide deep inside, thrust herself against him to find her own pleasure, felt her climax build and stretch toward release.

This is life, she thought, and cried out.

Ripley stood in the loading dock and looked at the people assembled in front of her, watched them absorb the information that Tully and Wilks laid out. They were in orbit around what sounded like hell.

The *Kurtz* would land and drop off the APC, in which some of them would go check things out, then report back. Everyone agreed that it was the best action before coming up with a final plan. To be certain of what they were up against.

Must be getting mellow with age, she thought. There was a time there when waiting to do anything would have been out of the question.

Moto had suggested sending a robot probe first, but the motion had been vetoed. Not a bad idea, but what probes they had were severely limited. It wouldn't pay to get the wrong idea, and if the bot you sent couldn't see very well or smell the alien stink, that might give you a false sense of security.

Ripley had to smile at that. Security. Right.

Wilks and Tully wrapped up their presentation and turned to look at Ripley. She knew what was expected of her.

"Well," she said. "Anyone dream of the queen last night?"

The crew members looked at each other and shook their heads. Apparently nobody had.

"Does that mean she knows we're here?" said Adcox.

"Maybe so. Or it could just mean that she overshot us. Hard to say."

Adcox nodded, as did several of the others.

"You know about this place," Ripley said. "I wouldn't ask anyone to do anything I'm not prepared to do myself, so I'll be on that APC—and I'm asking for volunteers. Most of you have been in combat situations, but some of you are physically stronger and have a better chance out there. You need to make the decision, not me.

"However, some of you will have to stay onboard the ship. Tully—you're our computer whiz, you stay here."

"I figured as much," Tully said. She tried to sound disappointed, but Ripley could see her relax a little.

Ripley continued. "McQuade and Brewster—as pilots, I don't see how we can risk losing either of you, since I'll be down there—"

Brewster cut in. "Hey, I'm ready for this! McQuade can fly the ship, I—"

"Look, I'm not saying you're not capable, Brewster. We need you here. Besides, there has to be somebody to pick up the pieces if we fuck up. Got it?"

"Yeah," he said, in a tone of voice that said he didn't get it at all.

Tough shit, thought Ripley.

"Jones, you stay here, too."

The doctor shrugged. "You might need me there," he said.

"That's true. But if we get hurt, we can use the aid kits. Better you're here where you can do major repairs in relative safety when we get back." *If we get back*, Ripley said to herself.

Falk stood up. "I'm going," he said.

Ripley had assumed that he would volunteer. She nodded at him. "Okay, Falk. Welcome aboard."

Dunston and Carvey stood at the same time. Adcox rose, as did Billie. Wilks stepped away from Tully and joined the others, followed by Ana Moto.

Ripley held up a hand. "Stop there," she said. "Like I said, we need a backup crew in case anything happens to us. And if we all go, there's no room for weapons. Moto, you stay; you're probably the best strategist. Billie—"

"I'm going," she said, voice calm.

The determination in the young woman's eyes was firm. Ripley hesitated, then nodded.

"All right," she said.

She turned to McQuade and gave him the go-ahead. He walked to the front of the group and started to explain how the loader suits worked.

Ripley looked at her crew. Good people, all of them. This could work, it just might work.

It *had* to work.

Wilks stood in the control room with McQuade, Brewster, and Tully, and watched them look at the readings on landing sites. They were twenty minutes from drop and he could feel adrenaline seep into his system when he looked through the shield. Once more he was going to face off with the monsters. As long as there were any of them left, or he could still breathe, that was gonna keep happening, but it didn't seem to get any easier. You'd think he'd be used to it by now.

Brewster picked up a cluster of erratic movement in the southern hemisphere, which coincided with Tully's reading of warmest temperature. They would head there first. No one was betting whether or not *she* would be there; everyone seemed to know.

The meeting had continued for a while after the APC team selection had been made. McQuade demonstrated the makeshift suits and Ripley gave a rundown on the scientist, Orona. Wilks had known about Orona and his bombs, as had Ana Moto. Funny—Ripley had seemed relieved that they knew.

It looked like a rough ride going down, and it would be pretty stupid if one of them got whacked by a coffee cup someone forgot to put away, so they policed the ship and dogged down everything loose.

Wilks had seen how Billie and Brewster had

looked at each other during the meeting, and again during load. He couldn't ignore those glances, and he had a pretty good idea what they meant.

Well, it wasn't his business. Then again, he couldn't ignore how it made him feel. That Billie and the corporal had made love—the thought of it made him grit his teeth. It felt . . . it was uncomfortable, although he couldn't pin down why exactly. Billie was a big girl, he didn't need to watch out for her—

That he thought about it now, a few minutes before they were to embark on the queen's home, was stupid. As if he didn't have enough to worry about. He shook his head a little and concentrated on the computer landscape in front of him. They were about to fly into a big fucking mess and he needed to be all the way there for it. Not concerned about Billie's sex life . . .

With effort, he pushed everything else out of his mind and took a deep breath. It was time to get down to business here, time to do what had to be done. Everything else was secondary. It was gonna be kick ass or get it kicked and either way, he was ready.

Semper fi, motherfuckers, and the devil take the last guy out of the trenches.

15

Moto pulled off her protective goggles and turned to Ripley.

"If that doesn't hold it shut, nothing will," she said.

Moto had just finished welding braces around one of the hold's two exit hatches. McQuade was still working on the other one. Ripley stood with her arms crossed and waited for the alloy's glow to die down. The air stank of burned metal and plastic.

They were going in a few minutes and the tension of the crew showed in their tight expressions, but Ripley felt surprisingly calm.

McQuade snapped off his welder. "Done," he said, a little too loudly.

Ripley nodded at him. She had thought she

would be a lot jumpier by now; her relaxed state was almost disconcerting. But it wasn't a lack of concern, it was more like . . .

Fulfillment, she thought. *Being where I'm supposed to be.*

After she checked the hatches, Ripley followed the other two back to the upper deck. The hatches looked solid enough and were certainly the best they could do—but this wasn't some drone. She would have to hope that the queen bitch wasn't going to be too much for them to handle. She had dealt with ordinary queens, and they were bigger, stronger, and meaner than drones. She hoped the queen of queens wasn't that much worse.

No matter. It was what they had.

Now the crew strapped into their seats.

Billie offered her a quick and nervous smile as Ripley walked to the front and around the control area's partition.

Brewster sat in pilot one, Tully behind him.

Wilks adjusted a strap on one of the secondary chairs.

Ripley moved up to pilot two and sat.

Wilks looked at her. "Hey, Ripley. We ran a matrix on the movement in the southern hemisphere, in case we have to land there—"

"No, 'in case,' " she said. "She's there. You know it."

Wilks shook his head and grinned. "Okay, *probably*. We'll know soon enough. Anyway, Tully picked up rock formations like you wouldn't believe. It's going to be tricky. There's a little wind, too."

Brewster turned from the console and nodded at Wilks. "If it was easy, anybody could do it. Besides, topography's the APC's problem. All I gotta do is drop you off."

Ripley let the bitterness slip past. Brewster was obviously still pissed that he wasn't going to attend their scouting party.

"Yeah, but flying it's going to be a bitch. Glad you're at the helm, Brewster. Hotshot like you shouldn't have too many problems."

Brewster didn't reply, but Ripley saw him relax slightly. Good. They were going into harm's way and the last thing she needed was a smarmy pilot.

Tully spoke up. "Carvey and I sectored the APC's comlink," she said, "so you don't have to worry about scattering."

"Great," said Ripley. She looked at the readouts in front of her and felt her hands start to clench. The lack of tension she'd felt wasn't going to last now that there was nothing left to do but sit and wait.

"I guess we're ready," she said.

"Good thing," said Brewster, " 'cause here we go, bearing oh-six—"

The rest of his words seemed to fade as he punched a button and they fell out of space.

Billie gripped the armrests of her chair, eyes tightly closed. Her stomach was knotted in the usual lurch of free-fall. This was a feeling she didn't think she'd ever get used to. She imagined the *Kurtz* shooting through the heavy clouds, pummeled by the rains and—

Scratch that, she thought as she felt nausea rise up. She searched for a more pleasant thought. *Last night with Dylan, the closeness, the touching, the rolling and pumping, over and over, falling forever*—oh Lord, scratch that, too.

The ship suddenly seemed to catch up to her twisted belly. Not an easy drop, but the worst had to be over. She opened her eyes. She hoped the worst was over.

Char smiled at her shakily. "Not dead yet," she said.

Billie nodded and looked over at the nearest port. Nothing to see; they were still too high.

Wilks leaned his head around the partition, expression tense. "Local winds look to be pushing 130 knots," he said. "And that's down below the jet stream. Better button up before it gets rough."

At the sound of his voice, Billie felt her guts tighten. *So much for the worst being over.*

She fought down a rising sense of dread.

She felt that her entire life had been spent in preparation for this moment. She believed in this, was ready to risk her neck for it—for Amy, for Ripley and Wilks and the others. They all had their own reasons. Duty. Honor. She looked over at Falk, at his blank face—he had vengeance. It wasn't the thought of death that frightened her, it was the uncertainty.

The flight smoothed out, became almost calm.

Carvey and Falk unbuckled and moved to one of the ports.

What the hell, Billie thought, and stood to join them.

They broke out of the cloud cover into the most desolate place Billie had ever seen. The *Kurtz* moved too fast to get a good look, but as far as she could tell, it was all the same.

Pools of shallow gray water stretched for klicks, broken up and surrounded by dirty humps of rock. Clumps of colorless vegetation, much of it apparently fungal, towered at the edges of the water. Some strange variety of beige moss seemed to cover everything. They passed a copse of the bizarre plant life, which struck Billie as the work of an insane sculptor. Twisted limbs and vines branched off into the air and pulsed slightly in the winds that shook the ship. Off in the distance, Billie saw impossibly-tall stands of rock scattered randomly in the endless dark sea. Nice place. She turned away.

"We'd better head down to the APC," she said.

"Right," said Carvey. He started toward the stairs, followed by Falk and Dunston.

Jones walked back toward medical.

Billie stood still for a moment, tried to prepare herself.

"You okay?" Char asked.

Billie looked at her friend, saw the concern on the lieutenant's face.

"Yeah. Just getting my nerve up."

As Billie walked behind Char to the lower level, she couldn't stop the fear from welling up. That they were all just part of some huge plan; that their sense of purpose was fake. That maybe they hadn't really come of their own accord, but had been lured by the dreams . . .

"Buddha, what a great place," said Brewster. "Maybe I'll take my vacation here." He navigated the *Kurtz* through the strange environment. Crosswinds buffeted the vessel hard enough to rock it.

Wilks stared. Yeah, this was without a doubt the most god-awful planet he'd ever seen. He could almost feel the thick wetness of the air around the ship, smell the dead chemical odor of the alkaline water. Just looking at this nightmare gave him the creeps.

Brewster interrupted his thoughts. "I got a spot scoped where it seems relatively calm, not far from the main cluster of movement."

No one spoke for a minute.

"Take it or leave it, folks—I can't dick around for long in this damn wind," said Brewster.

"Take it," said Ripley, and stood up. "Come on, Wilks, let's go back with the grunts."

Tully smiled at them as they headed down the stairs. "Luck," she said.

Brewster struggled with the controls but managed a thumbs-up.

The others were crowded around the APC in the dock. Wilks motioned for the rest of the crew to get on, and boarded last.

He watched everyone strap in before he moved to the front. Billie sat at the console; she would monitor outside activity as they got closer to the motion Brewster had picked up.

A voice crackled out over the intercom.

"Hey, kids, almost there," said Brewster. "Tully says the movement has stopped, but it seemed to be coming from a formation almost due west from where we're dropping you—that's a two-seven-two heading, to be exact."

"Rock formation?" said Billie.

"Negative. Looks organic. Listen, Carvey, you still owe me money, so be careful, okay? Goes for the rest of you, too."

"Got it," said Billie.

"Thanks, Brewster," Wilks said. "On your go."

Wilks keyed the controls for the machine and checked the navigational. Everything looked fine. The mobile unit was built like a chunk of lead on wheels, designed to move over any terrain, if not comfortably, at least efficiently. The front viewscreen gave a good shot of the outside; currently, the inside of the dock. There was also a small kleersteel shield that offered a more limited view.

There were recoilless guns mounted on the pivotal up top, as well as in the front. This was supposed to be a check—with any luck, he wouldn't have to use them.

"Stand by," said Brewster, in a burst of static.

Wilks tensed, ready.

The *Kurtz* touched down. Wilks rolled his head with the sudden impact, felt the planet surface grind and crunch beneath the ship. The APC slid forward as the deck dropped out on metal struts, the hatch opening outward.

"Go!"

Wilks grabbed the control stick and eased the

APC off the extended ramp and into the water. There were scattered rocks and weird vegetable growths here and there, but essentially they were looking at an ocean less than a meter deep. Here, anyway. It surrounded them in every direction as far as he could see. Wind rippled the surface into a shifting washboard, occasional gusts blowing spray from the tiny whitecaps.

The APC's rear wheels pulled off the deck and they settled into the liquid with scarcely a bump.

"Good job," said Wilks. "We're down. And welcome to town, folks."

"And *we* are outta here," said Brewster.

The sounds of the ship as it lifted were loud even inside the APC. Brewster and the others would head back up, above the winds, and wait for the pickup call.

If there's anybody left to send it, thought Wilks. There was something wrong, he felt it in his gut; but they were there, and it was time.

"Let's go see if the queen's home," he said.

The APC rumbled forward.

16

From the position of the cam on the APC, it was nearly impossible to tell exactly what it was they were headed toward. The screen showed nothing but water and sky, close enough in color to be nearly indistinguishable. It was like moving through a void.

Billie mostly kept her gaze on the motion sensors and the Doppler screen, where she had something to report: "We got six roughly spherical objects, approximately twenty meters apart and arranged in a circle. Largest measures maybe thirty meters high; it's centered inside the others," she said.

"Sounds like Adcox's nest," said Wilks.

"Yeah," Billie said. She pushed her hair off her sweaty forehead. The APC's coolers could only do so much against the wet heat of the planet that pressed in on them.

They wobbled and bumped as the APC made its way slowly through the water.

"Level, my ass," Wilks said. "I'd like to see Brewster's idea of rough terrain."

It all felt like a dream to Billie, and her heart thumped hard and loud enough she was surprised nobody noticed.

"Wilks—this is supposed to be a scouting trip, right? Why are we headed straight to her nest? Shouldn't we find somewhere safer, to observe—"

"Look around. Where would you suggest?"

"I'm just saying that we can scope things out a little more thoroughly, try a probe—"

"Listen, kid, we're not going to drive this thing into her front door, we're just going to pull up nearby and see what happens, okay? If the probes we had were worth a shit, I'd send one, but none of the robots we got can do the job."

Billie nodded, but continued to worry. "It doesn't feel good, Wilks," she said.

His lips tightened. "Yeah," he said. "I copy that."

Billie sighed. She and Wilks had been here before. Not this place, but this kind of situation. Somehow that felt a little comforting. Between the two of them, they'd pulled off some pretty scary deals. "ETA, two minutes," she said.

"We'll be ready," Ripley called out from behind her.

Billie wanted to go back and talk to Ripley

about her fear. Maybe there was some kind of psychic thing going on.

Suddenly the APC ground to a halt with a jarring crunch. The unit tilted to the left, throwing Billie back into her chair.

"What the fuck—?" began Falk.

Ripley held up her hand for silence. "Wilks, Billie, what do we have?"

Billie ran the diagnostic. "We bent one of the aft axle struts, but I think that's it," said Billie. Her voice sounded shaky.

"What did we hit?" said Adcox.

Wilks called out over his shoulder. "Don't know. Something underwater; treads lifted and we lost traction. Hang on, let me see if we can rock back off it."

The APC's engines rumbled. It took a few seconds, but Wilks managed to pull free of the obstruction. "Okay, we're clear." Then, "Take a look at the screen."

Ripley looked up at the vid screen and inhaled sharply as the picture panned left.

"Oh, my God," Adcox said.

They were less than a hundred meters from a huge, round orb sitting in the murky water, pinkish gray in color, with strange lines crisscrossing the surface.

Like veins, thought Ripley.

A long, thick cord connected it to another orb, larger. The one they were closest to was the length of the APC and maybe twice as high.

"I think we ran over something connected to that thing," said Wilks.

"Billie, is anybody home?" Ripley asked.

"No movement. If they're around, they must be asleep. Look, I think we should back off a little. I don't feel so great about this."

Ripley frowned. "We're here. If they heard that knock and they're still not coming, I think we'll be all right for a minute."

They all watched the screen with intense concentration.

Nothing happened.

Ripley half-expected to see a horde of the giant insects launch themselves from behind the weird orbs and attack. She looked at Billie; the girl was watching the sensor readouts closely.

No movement . . .

It was Falk who broke the silence. "Let's go have a peek, what say?" He stood, picked up a comset, hooked it over the back of his head, and reached for a boot to one of the mechano suits.

Dunston also stood.

Ripley shook her head. "I think we should wait, maybe nudge one of them with the APC first," she said. "We don't know what we're dealing with here."

Falk continued to suit up. "Isn't that why we came?" he said. "To find out?"

Carvey got up and helped Dunston buckle on one of the lift boots before he grabbed a third suit.

"It's a good idea," said Carvey. "We'll just hop out and have a look. We've got weapons, we're armored, and the APC's right here. We're out there five minutes, tops."

Ripley thought about it. They knew what the aliens were capable of; they weren't going to be charging out there ignorant of what could happen. And Carvey had a point—they were as prepared as they were going to get. It was no crazier than the whole mission, which made less sense every time she thought about it.

"Okay," she said.

"No," said Billie from behind them. "Ripley, don't let them go, this isn't going to work. Can't you feel it?"

Dunston stepped forward, awkward in the suit. Hydraulics whined, the boots clumped heavily as he moved. "Billie," he said, his voice calm. "This is a choice. We made the decision to come here. This is part of it."

Something in his face, perhaps the acceptance of fate, stopped Billie from protesting any further. She turned and moved back to the front without another word.

The three men, fully suited, stood by the door and looked to Ripley for their cue. They each wore thick vests with head protectors, jointed metal running the length of their limbs. Each carried standard military carbines, the same 10mm caseless weapons Ripley had learned to use.

"Listen to your sets," she said. "Billie is monitoring the cluster. Any sign of trouble, get back here; we don't want any dead heroes. Good luck."

She paused for a moment. *What else is there to say?* Nothing.

"Go," she said.

The hatch slid open.

Wilks felt the blast of damp heat as the door slid shut. The smell was like he'd imagined, but worse—like rotten, poisoned food. The wind made the exposed edges of the hatch whistle.

He breathed through clenched teeth and watched the screen. Billie was pallid and tense beside him, but she also watched the readouts carefully.

Wilks wished he were out there with the others, but he tried to let it go. He was the best APC driver they had, and if anything went wrong they'd want to leave in a hurry.

"Falk, talk to me," he said.

"We're moving toward it, maybe thirty meters away now. We'll stay on this side of it." Falk's transmission was clear.

"Christo, it fucking *stinks*," said Carvey. "You're missing out, Sarge."

"What are you bitching about? At least you can breathe."

"Wish I'd thought to bring a kite. Wind must be gusting to a hundred klicks out here."

"One-fifteen," Wilks said.

He watched as the three men appeared at the bottom of the viewscreen. "Okay, now we got you on visual," he said.

One of the figures turned and waved. "Hi, Ma!"

Wilks grinned. "Knock that shit off, Carvey,

you're supposed to be part of a crack scouting team here."

Trying to be funny to break the tension seemed a little strained, but it was something.

The figures approached the sphere. Their boots rose and fell in the muck that came up to their knees, spatters of it blowing away in the gusts.

They separated a few meters from the orb; Falk remained in front while Dunston and Carvey moved to the sides.

"Don't get too far apart," said Wilks. The three men stopped. "Stay in sight of each other."

"There's goop all over this thing," said Carvey. "Like, uh—jelly."

"Seems to be emanating from the formation's core." That from Dunston.

"What *are* these things?" Carvey said. "They're too big to be egg sacs.... I *hope* they're too big to be egg sacs. Whatever the hell it is, it's oozing like a sonofabitch. I can almost see inside—" He raised a mechanical limb to touch it.

Billie gasped and Wilks felt his heart catch.

"Oh, fuck, movement!" she said.

"Everybody get out of there *now*!" Wilks shouted.

"It's coming from inside the pods!" said Billie into the com. "Move, get away!"

The three figures on the screen stumbled back as the nearest pod opened like a giant egg sac and a huge, glistening shape rose from out of it.

Adcox cried out from behind them. A queen-sized drone, bigger than any Wilks had ever seen, snapped out one powerful claw so fast Carvey hardly saw it move and latched on to his head protector.

The monster raised Carvey into the air like a child with a toy.

"Falk, Jesus, get it off, get it off me—!"

Carvey's cries were cut off abruptly as the drone used its other claw and ripped his throat out. The creature tossed the handful of flesh away and pulled one of Carvey's arms off. Tossed that away, too.

Oh, fuck—!

So goddamned fast!

Dunston and Falk had barely gotten their weapons raised.

"We're coming!" Ripley yelled into her 'com, but the two men were already slogging quickly backward toward the APC. "Go, Wilks! I'm on the guns!"

Falk blasted at the drone. It dropped Carvey, screamed, and started toward him, hissing, then fell into the water as Dunston's carbine joined the fire. They might be bigger and faster than normal drones, but they could die.

Wilks jammed the APC into full throttle.

Billie slammed her fist against the console. "Fuck, oh fuck, the other pods!"

Ripley was bringing the APC's guns online when she heard Billie.

"Come *on*!" she shouted to Wilks.

The APC lurched forward—only to hit another stop. The engine whined noisily.

"Dunston!" It was Falk yelling.

Ripley looked up at the viewscreen as an alien leaped *over* one of the pods and pounced at the teacher. He fell onto his back with a splash, absorbed the shock of the huge drone, and slammed his weapon into its belly—

Falk struggled to get a clear shot as the APC suddenly moved forward again—

"Die!" shouted Dunston.

Nothing happened. His weapon must have jammed. He raised his free arm, used the mechanical clamp to hold the alien's head away from his own—

It shrieked and opened its gigantic jaws. With a jerk, it shoved its head forward.

The steel armor crumpled like paper as its inner mouth snapped out and speared Dunston's face. Bright red splashed into the water and the teacher fell limp.

"Motherfucker!" yelled Falk, and opened up on the drone. The crash of gunfire shredded the alien. The area around the fallen creature hissed and bubbled as its blood ate the water. What fell on Dunston didn't matter.

Falk disappeared from the screen as the APC came to a stop.

"Wilks!" shouted Ripley.

"Don't make me knock, for Christ's sake!" said Falk through the 'com.

Adcox stood behind the door, weapon raised. Billie slammed the entry button and Falk fell inside, gasping.

"Close it!" he said.

Ripley caught a glimpse of one of the creatures

moving quickly through the muck. She put the gun tracker on it—

Billie slammed the hatch button again. "Come on—!"

The monster loped closer, its limbs splashing the foul water against the front of the APC—

Ripley said, "Too close to shoot, it'll spatter all over the APC—!"

The hatch closed.

"Emergency dustoff, now!" said Billie. She held her comlink headset in place with shaky fingers.

"We can't put down at your current position," said Brewster. His voice was anguished. "We got a force three hurricane wind aloft right there. Get away from the nest, get back closer to the initial drop point!"

"Shit!" Billie said.

"Billie, are you okay? Where's—"

"No time, Brewster," said Wilks. "Get moving. We'll be there ASAP."

Billie discommed and turned to Wilks. The aliens were so much bigger and stronger than before—

Before she could speak, something hammered against the APC wall, hard enough to dent metal.

Billie scanned the readouts. "Three of them," she said.

The entire unit was lifted and tipped backward, before it fell forward with a crash. The vid screen went black and mud splashed the kleersteel window. Metal groaned. Something snapped with a bell-like crack.

"Wilks," Billie said, in barely a whisper. She looked at the readout without blinking, hoped that it was wrong.

"Our internal cooling system just opened—" Even as she watched, the temperature was going up. "It's going to get hot in here. Crappy warranty on these things."

Wilks checked the monitor. "Ripley, we got some problems up here."

There was no answer.

Ripley belted the vest and nearly fell when the APC tipped. She picked up Falk's gun and checked the ammo read. Wilks shouted something at her as she searched the floor for additional magazines. Everything was rolling; the clips slid under the supply compartment.

"Ripley!" yelled Wilks again.

She walked to the front in the bulky suit. Falk and Adcox leaned against the wall that faced the door, weapons ready.

"Fuck this," said Falk. "Let's burn outta here."

Wilks turned around in his seat. He looked Ripley up and down. "Jesus," he said. "You're crazy."

"Just head for the drop site—"

"Can't. The manuals are shot, steering just about locked. Our reactor took a knock—we can go straight for about ten minutes and then we're talking meltdown. Got any ideas?"

"Yeah," said Ripley. "Use the APC's guns and hammer those three outside; won't matter if the acid damages the APC now. Seal the hatch and take off full speed as soon as I'm out. I need a couple minutes to get to her nest."

"And what are you going to do when you get there? Invite her to fucking tea?" said Wilks.

"I didn't come this far just to let her slip away," said Ripley. "If I can't capture her, I can kill her. I have to try. Listen, it's been good working with you—"

"You are fucking crazy," said Billie.

Ripley grinned and walked back to the rear hatch of the APC. Adcox followed, prepared to cover her.

Wilks triggered the APC's guns. One of them was still operable. The uranium slugs shattered the attacking aliens. "Clear," he said. "At the moment."

"Good luck," Ripley said.

The hatch opened and Ripley jumped out.

17

I'm showing several forms moving at high speed toward the APC," Billie said. Her mouth was dry. In spite of the heat, she felt cold all over. The blips on the screen wavered and jumped, moved closer.

"I guess that means Ripley's plan is working," she said.

Wilks didn't spare her a glance as he wrestled with the controls. "Reactor halfway to critical, APC's about to be overcome by superbugs—yeah, I'd say it's working. Any better and we could blow our brains out now and save those bastards the trouble."

"Should I call the *Kurtz* again?"

"Not yet. We give Ripley her five-plus and keep

going till this sucker suffers from a complete engine or axle lock."

"Then?" She turned to look at him. Her vision was blurred from sweat.

"Haven't gotten that far yet," he said.

The APC rocked. Billie looked back at the sensor and then screamed.

"Jesus—" said Wilks. A giant, dripping alien grin appeared on the other side of the kleersteel. The creature lifted huge, clawed hands up to the window, and with a muffled shriek plunged its head through the shield. The clear metal shattered inward, sprayed everywhere as the alien reached for Billie—

Ripley fell into the shallow water, grunted, and jumped up into a crouch. She tried to look in all directions at once, managed one; there was no immediate danger.

She didn't believe that the drones would have left their queen unprotected, but the only motion around her was the gently swaying ocean.

Doesn't mean it's going to stay that way ...

All of her senses were in overdrive. The putrid odor of the planet, combined with the heat and gravity, made her dizzy. Along with the fading sound of the APC, there was only the slosh of the water against her legs. The fierce winds had suddenly dwindled to almost nothing.

An alien's cry echoed through the dead air, but it came from the direction of the retreating transport.

She turned and faced the cluster of nests.

"It's just you and me, now," she said.

Wilks grabbed for his weapon.

The creature already had its claws on Billie. It hissed, its decayed breath filling the air as Wilks came up with his carbine. Everything was mired in time, creaking forward in slow motion and thick gravity. . . .

Too late, too late, his brain chanted.

The explosion thundered in his ears. The drone seemed to fly backward with a cry of rage and pain. Acid spattered, bubbled and smoked on the shards of kleersteel.

Adcox stepped forward, weapon extended. The alien was gone.

"Oh, *shit*," said Billie.

"Okay?" said Adcox.

Billie looked down at her ripped shirt and then back at the lieutenant. "Yeah."

Wilks exhaled heavily and checked the motion sensor. "One down," he said.

Hot, noxious air washed over them. Billie had a small cut on her left arm from the kleersteel, but that was it. That they hadn't been drenched with the bug's acid was amazing. . . .

Time to think about it later, Wilks told himself. He glanced at the APC readout to see the core temperature still rising.

"Keep your eye on that thing," he said.

If there is a later, he thought.

• • •

Ripley slowly splashed toward the orbs. She heard shots in the distance.

"Bet we got one of your babies," she said. Her muscles were sore from the gravity; it felt like a hundred kilos had been strapped to each limb. Even breathing was an effort. But she could *feel* the queen, the powerful aura of the bitch—

Water splashed behind her. Ripley spun, raised her weapon—

The drone was still twenty meters away. It screamed, opened its jaws—

Ripley pulled the trigger, fired a quick burst at the massive target's chest. The running creature stopped dead, its abdomen peeled outward by the explosive force of the rounds. It fell into the water, hissing like a punctured air tank. The wave motion rocked Ripley's legs and she fought to maintain balance. The noise of the shots hurt her ears. Should have worn plugs—

Another shriek to her left. She turned again. This one was closer and moved at incredible speed, even in the heavy gravity.

She fired twice.

The giant alien fell backward, its taloned feet in the air for a second before it rolled over. The thing's jointed tail flailed up and then lashed into the water before it lay still. Speckles of liquid splashed Ripley's face.

She crouched for a minute and listened: only the sizzle of alien blood as it dispersed into the water.

She faced the nest.

"Is that the best you can do?" she said, breathing hard. "Those are your chosen protectors?"

Silence.

"Why don't you show yourself?" Ripley whacked the arm of her mechanical suit against one of the connecting cords. It rippled and swayed slightly. She felt a bitter anger rise up. . . .

"What the fuck is this? Why don't you come out here and tell me?"

She hit the cord again and moved closer to the center orb.

"Explain the crew of the *Nostromo*. The *Sulaco*. Explain Earth! Explain my *daughter*, you bitch!"

Ripley waited, breathing hard.

Suddenly, the huge sphere jerked. The translucent goo quivered. A long crack appeared at the top of the thing, pulsing slightly. It started opening.

Ripley tapped her 'com, never taking her eyes off of the nest. "*Kurtz*, this is Ripley," she said quickly. "Zero my position and get your asses here."

Brewster's fuzzy voice spoke into her ear. "I told Wilks, the wind—"

"The wind has died down. Get that ship over my coordinates, *now*."

As she spoke, a blackness started to move up from the orb. A glossy, elongated shape, a skull easily two meters in length, raised up. Three clawed digits wrapped over the lip of the crack, and then another three. The queen slowly pulled herself up. She hissed at Ripley, drool falling from her jaws as she unfurled herself from her home.

The queen. The mama of all mamas. Come to receive her visitor.

She was at least eight meters long, her whipping, bony tail making her eight more. Her comb was sleek and wet. Several of her vertebrae arched outward like spines, ran down her back like a row of fingers. She had four arms. She was the biggest living creature Ripley had ever seen, taller than the elephant she'd seen in the zoo as a kid. Jesus.

The queen ducked her head forward and down, craned her obscene skull to get a better look at what had disturbed her.

"That's right," said Ripley. She backed away from the advancing creature. "Come on out and have a look."

"Core temperature's going up. Meltdown in—seven minutes," said Billie. Her body was still shaking, but she had managed to control the worst of it.

"We're talking more than meltdown," said Wilks. "When that core burns through to the liquid fuel chamber, we're looking at an explosion."

"Gee, and everything's been going *great* so far," Char said.

Wilks pushed at the controls and then sighed. "Well, the engine and the wheels still work," he said. "That means this thing probably keeps rolling until it blows. Time to leave this party; we'll have to make the drop site on foot."

"That's *fucked*," Char said.

"Take all the ammunition you can carry and move out. Unless you want to cook here."

"New readings at the outer perimeter," Billie said.

She squinted at the motion sensor and then tapped the side of it, hard. "There's a *wall* of them, Wilks!"

Even as she spoke, a dozen or so lights flashed on the screen.

"What—?" Char said. "They're running past us!"

"Mama is calling her children," Wilks said.

Billie could barely fathom the number of moving creatures it would take to give that reading.

"There must be thousands," she said. Her stomach knotted tighter. "Ripley."

"She'll do what she has to," said Wilks. He stood and walked to the back.

Billie and Char both looked through the open shield for a few seconds, the choking air fetid against their faces. The army of drones moved toward them like a sheet of rain, closer and closer. Dozens ran past the APC, headed back to the queen. Billie could hear their shrieks over the rising whine of the transport.

"It's almost certain suicide to get out," Char said. "And what happened to the nice breeze we had?"

"We *know* it's suicide to stay," Billie said. "Maybe the bastards are on autopilot or something and they won't even notice us."

Without another word, they walked back to Falk and Wilks. The two men handed them loaded weapons and extra clips. They all moved to the rear hatch.

"Conserve ammo," said Wilks, "and fire only at targets coming at us. Stay close."

Billie searched for something to say, some last words, but there was nothing. Wilks hit the button and jumped, slipped, landed on his shoulder with a splash.

A chorus of howls went up all around the APC as Billie took a breath and leaped.

Ripley continued to back away from the hissing queen. It seemed like a long fucking time before she heard a noise that drowned the bitch out.

The sound of the *Kurtz* moving in overhead was sweet music.

"We'll bring her in as low as we can," crackled Brewster through her 'com, "and then—holy *shit*."

"Quite the prize," said Ripley. "Open the containment chamber and get close to me."

"Yeah," said Brewster. "But if that wind picks up again ..."

The queen refocused her attention on the thundering ship. She backed away from Ripley a step and let out a high-pitched, mewling noise.

"Pretty ship," said Ripley. "See the nice, pretty ship." She darted her gaze quickly to the descending *Kurtz* and then back to the queen. "Bitch want to go for a ride on the pretty ship?"

The queen didn't offer a reply.

"Closer, Brewster, come *on*."

The queen took another step backward,

wagged her huge head, looked at Ripley, then the ship.

The *Kurtz*'s cargo bay was directly over her, the hatch open. Keeping her weapon pointed at the queen, Ripley held her other arm up. The clamp on the suit opened and then closed on metal.

She pulled herself up. It took a tremendous effort. Her arm felt like it was going to jerk out of its socket, even with the suit's augmentation.

The alien watched but didn't try to follow her.

As big as the ship was, Ripley couldn't believe the monster was afraid. Curious, perhaps, but the goddamned things never seemed to be afraid of anything.

Ripley sidled into the dock on her elbows, scrabbled forward on her knees.

She stood and looked down at the queen.

The creature hissed at her. All of her metallic teeth glinted wetly in the dim light.

Ripley smiled. "Perfect, Brewster. Hold here for a minute."

She retrained her weapon at the closest orb and fired.

The queen screamed as pieces of her nest flew. Ripley kept the trigger depressed, sent a steady stream of bullets into the orb. Bits of the weird, fleshy material dropped into the water and sank.

She released the trigger. The queen turned from the remains of her broken home and howled in anger. She looked at Ripley.

She knows I'm doing it, Ripley thought. Knows

what a gun is even though she's never seen one before.

Watch this.

Ripley aimed at the next orb and opened fire. With a shriek, the queen leaped at her.

Ripley stumbled backward as the queen extended her huge claws toward the slick alloy. The alien grasped at the edge of the door's frame and caught hold.

"Up, now, up!" Ripley screamed into the 'com.

The *Kurtz* lifted.

The queen pulled herself into the dock as Ripley ran toward the inner door.

"Seal the outer hatch!"

The queen screamed a sound of absolute fury as she started toward Ripley.

Ripley spun back to look at the queen and the nearly closed hatch. She had to be sure—

The queen's dark tail lashed out and the tip of it reached Ripley by the door. It thrashed down, thumped against the protecting bars of the mechano suit, bent the metal and stacked carbon fibers, smashed into Ripley's skull. The force of the blow knocked her sprawling.

The chamber washed out. Tiny bursts of light flashed around the howling alien. Ripley shook her head as the queen turned away from her, leaped at the hatch, and pounded on it. The trapped monster screamed for her freedom.

The shrill sound faded as Ripley scrabbled backward and the world went to gray.

•   •   •

Wilks, Billie, Adcox, and Falk stood in a circle and faced outward. Scores of the drones loped past them without stopping, splashed through the shallow water toward their mother. If the cloying, chemical stench of rot, the heavy air, and the heat weren't bad enough, hundreds of the nightmare creatures streamed past them, making it closer to hell than Wilks ever thought he'd be.

Someone fired from behind him. Aliens screamed and hissed and kept running.

One of the drones veered toward him, reached out, claws hooked—

Wilks squeezed the trigger and sprayed the alien with a short burst.

The thing fell into the water. Three or four of the bugs stumbled over the dead creature but kept running.

Another monster howled, lunged at Wilks. He fired again.

Falk cursed steadily behind him as more of the creatures stopped and were killed.

Wilks knew they would never make the drop site. There was no way they could move amidst the army of mindless bugs and keep themselves covered. He aimed at one of the grinning drones as it looked in their direction and squeezed off a single round. The alien's head exploded. It collapsed into the water, which bubbled madly now with the acidic blood of its brothers.

"We're not going to make it!" Billie shouted.

Wilks pointed his weapon at another one and fired. "Five more minutes and the APC will detonate," he called back. "We'll fucking take them with us!"

He squeezed the trigger over and over and hoped that their ammo would last until the white heat of the APC ended it all. . . .

The queen's tail lashed at Ripley's leg, slapped it hard enough to move the pain from her head. Her eyes snapped open. She had crumpled against the wall next to the door when—

My head, she thought. The queen still thrashed wildly at the outer hatch, but it wasn't giving.

Ripley hit the button that would get her out of danger. The door into the APC bay slid open.

At the sound, the queen turned. With her tail coiled behind her, she prepared to leap—

Ripley fell into the clean air of the dock and jerked her legs after her. Moto stood there, welder in hand.

"Quick!"

Moto slammed the control. The door closed a split second before the queen barreled into it. A muffled pounding started on the other side, but the reinforced metal held.

Ripley leaned against the wall and watched Moto seal the entry. She never thought she would think the canned air of the ship was sweet, but it was; she was alive—!

And the queen was *hers*!

"Going for a ride, bitch."

McQuade stepped forward and helped Ripley pull off the leggings of the suit. "Christo, Ripley, you did it!" he said.

Ripley winced as he pulled the metal boot off her left leg. "Yeah. Hurry, we have to go get the others!"

Moto finished the door and stood. She and McQuade exchanged a look.

"Can't," said McQuade. "Brewster says we're getting the hell out of here."

"What are you talking about?" said Ripley. "They're dead?" She suddenly felt dizzy and pressed a hand to her forehead.

"No. The APC's gone critical—it'll blow in a few minutes. The squad's pinned down in one of the narrow valleys, and Brewster said it's too tight for pickup—"

Ripley ran to the stairs before McQuade finished. Moto and the captain followed. She clambered up, ignored her body's mute cries of pain as she climbed into the control room.

Brewster and Tully sat at the console, expressions grim.

"Ripley," said Brewster. "Glad you're—"

"Get to those people, *now*!"

"Look, there's no way! I wish to God there was, but the wind is rising, there's no goddamn room, and no time!"

"Find a way," she said. "If we die, we die. What if it was you down there?"

Brewster frowned. "Listen—" he began.

"No, *you* listen. You take it back or I will." She was still in the top half of the suit and the servos whined as she snapped the grippers shut.

He blew out a big breath. "Fuck it." He nodded. "Okay," he said. "Hold on."

•   •   •

"Less than a hundred rounds here!" Char yelled.

Falk cursed and threw his weapon down. "Dry!"

Billie moved closer to him and covered. Her head ached and pounded with the endless sound of explosions and shrieks. The air beat down on her, the world had become screams and death and it was too much trouble just to stand up—

She hoped Ripley had made it, that it wasn't all for nothing. She felt tears roll down her cheeks. A huge emptiness opened inside her gut as she took out another of the slavering aliens. She had been here before and she hadn't gotten *used* to it, but she wasn't as afraid as she had been the last time. Fuck it.

The creatures suddenly scattered, backed away from their small group. Hundreds of them howled at once, reached their arms up to the sky. It was deafening. Billie turned to Wilks, confused—

He pointed upward, a tight grin on his scarred face.

The *Kurtz*! She hadn't heard the engines, her ears overwhelmed with the alien shrieks and gunfire.

Wilks grabbed her roughly, jerked her from under the drop path of the approaching ship.

The aliens screamed, ran toward the descending vessel. Dozens of them were crushed into the murky liquid, smashed into the mud under the weight.

The planet rumbled beneath her feet. A wave of

the foul ocean rose up, knocked into them at chest level. Char fell, but Falk caught her; Wilks kept an arm around Billie and leaned into the wave. He fired at a drone that ran toward them.

The APC bay door was open. Ripley and Moto stood on either side of the dock, holding on to metal struts. They pointed weapons past the four of them and fired continuously.

Billie and Wilks ran toward the dock. Billie saw Ripley, was relieved to see she was okay. But then Ripley's mouth formed into a scream. As they stumbled into the bay, Billie looked over her shoulder. The aliens were running into the suppressive fire and falling to the sides of the ship by the score. Falk was right behind them, but—

One of the drones had grabbed Char. She had fallen forward, with an alien right behind her. As in some vicious parody of sex, it pushed against her, shoved her face into the water. Billie saw it plunge a claw through the back of Char's neck, watched it force her head back up. Her blood was startlingly red against the gray water. Her head flopped to the side, hung by shreds of her flesh.

The alien's cry of triumph was short as bullets cut it in half—but Charlene Adcox was dead.

Hundreds of the drones threw themselves at the closing lock as Ripley and Moto hosed their fire through the narrowing gap. Just before it shut completely, a lunging creature stuck one clawed hand into the bay. The lock cycled shut and cut two of the drone's fingers off. They sizzled and hissed on the floor of the ship, burned smoking craters in the flooring.

They were all pressed to the floor of the dock as the ship suddenly bounced and rocketed upward.

"Brace yourselves—the APC will blow in a few seconds!" Ripley yelled. The words sounded far away. Wilks had hooked one arm around a metal beam and held tightly to Billie with the other.

Billie didn't hear the explosion, but the ship rocked violently around them. It tilted to one side, yawed impossibly. Billie and Wilks crashed sidelong into the wall.

And then it was over. The *Kurtz* straightened itself, smoothed out. Only the drone of the engines broke the silence.

Billie took a huge gulp of air and began to sob against Wilks's chest. He stroked her hair gently and didn't let go.

"It's okay. We made it. It's okay."

Once again they had outrun death.

18

Wilks pushed the gray bar up with a grunt and slowly lowered it to his chest. He exhaled, raised it again.

He was alone in the *Kurtz*'s small gym. Falk had been there when he had walked in; the big man had nodded at him once, acknowledged his presence without a word, and left for the showers. Wilks understood. Their success with the capture was overshadowed by the deaths of three good people. No one wanted to talk about it.

The decision to put off deepsleep for a few days hadn't needed discussion; they were only one day from the mother's planet and the crew needed time to digest what had happened. Time didn't move in sleep, after all.

Wilks set the bar back on lock and stood,

reached for the smaller hand weights to work his pecs. He was already on his second set; his muscles trembled slightly as he extended his arms and brought them in. But the body fatigue could be ignored. Concentrating on workouts helped, a little. The sweat that dripped from his skin washed away some of the feelings. Anger. Sorrow. The guilt that had chased him for so long, that he was still alive, for what it was worth. A career marine who would never make it past sergeant, who couldn't save the people who looked to him—

Billie had holed up in her quarters alone. Wilks had gone to see her the night before and again this morning and had brought her something to eat.

She had been listless, unresponsive. Her initial outburst of tears in the APC dock hadn't been repeated. He had searched for something to say to drive that haunted look from her eyes, but what? He could almost see her replay the death of the lieutenant over and over as she stared at the wall. Her friend. Her friend who she undoubtedly had felt responsible for.

Wilks had saved Billie's life more than once, and she his—but to save her from guilt? That was more than he could do for himself. So he sat and watched her until the frustration had been so great that he had excused himself, come here.

Coward, his mind whispered. *Fucking coward.*

Another part of him spoke up. *Hey, I'm not a shrink! I'm just a marine. . . .*

Yeah. Right.

He sighed heavily and moved back to the leg

machine. Maybe a third set would pound his brain into submission.

Billie sat on her bed and tried not to think. They were in space, the mother alien was quiet in the hold, they were on their way to kill the brood on Earth and save Amy—

—*who is probably dead, like Char, like Carvey and Dunston, killed, murdered, dead*—

She pressed her hands to her forehead and waited for tears to come. No chance. She didn't deserve the release, and the sadness was too big. That they had been so close to the *Kurtz*, inches from safety ...

Carvey and Dunston, too. Brewster's best friend and the man who had been a teacher, who had convinced her that he had made a choice. To die. She hadn't known either of them as well as she had Char. Charlene. Billie had asked her on the trip that had cost her her life.

Wilks had been to see her, twice. She had tried to eat after he had gone, but the food stuck in her throat. Wilks's usually unreadable face had spoken plenty. She knew that he wanted to help, to make it better for her, but of course there was nothing to be said. They all had their own guilt.

Dylan Brewster had come last night after Wilks had gone, to explain that it should have been him, not Carvey. That Carvey had never been a "real" marine—his friend had been a kid at heart, eager to please. Hell, Carvey had only come on this trip *because* of Brewster—

Billie understood his pain, but was alone in her own.

She had not asked him to stay.

She tried to be objective, to tell herself that Char had made her own decision. That was true—and it didn't matter, because she was gone.

She'd thought she had come for Amy, but it was really about saving herself. Char Adcox had come to deal with her own loss, and Billie's reasons seemed selfish in comparison. Would the end justify the means? How could she know? Maybe the aliens were meant to have Earth; who was she to fuck with fate?

Billie lay down and pulled the coverlet up to her chin. Maybe later she would go talk to Ripley. But not now.

Ripley sat leaning against the dock wall next to the containment chamber and listened. Every now and then the queen rustled, a sliding, clicking noise as she moved her sharp body against the smooth, alloyed interior of her prison.

Ripley had spent most of the night here; the queen had eventually tired of pounding and screaming in the early hours of morning. Ripley checked the navigational comp and set McQuade to work on repairs—the damage to the *Kurtz* had been minimal. Jones tried to get her to medlab, but she was fine. And she had wanted to listen to the queen beat uselessly against the walls for a while.

Ripley was sorry about the deaths of Dunston and Carvey and Adcox; they had all died to get the queen to the *Kurtz*, and she knew that a large part of the responsibility was on her shoulders. But she would have died, too, had it been called for. To wipe out the murderous breed, the bitch queen who had caused the deaths of so many . . .

The fleeting desire she'd had to blow the queen into a million pieces when she could have was nothing compared to her hatred. The rage was hot and temporary; her hatred was cold and hard and forever. The bastards' extermination would vindicate all she had become.

She knew that living a life for revenge was not a healthy way to exist. She didn't care. This was right, she felt it stronger with every passing moment; each hour was a step closer to fulfillment.

The empty bay in front of her suddenly doubled. Ripley blinked several times. The double vision cleared.

Her head still ached where the bitch's tail had slapped her, but it was minor. The huge bruise on her leg already seemed to be fading. She was just tired, and hadn't eaten lately—

The thought of food and sleep was appealing. She stood and walked away from the door to the chamber.

"Later, you shit," she called out over her shoulder.

As she started toward the stairs, she noticed that the ship seemed to tilt slightly to the right. She frowned and paused, reached one hand out to touch the wall. The gravity wasn't supposed to flicker like that, she thought, taking another step toward the ladder. Suddenly, she felt like she was standing on the wall. She leaned into it, tried to right the effect.

"Tully!" she shouted.

No response.

Something was horribly wrong. She saw the alarm button on the wall and reached for it.

Why hasn't it gone off already—?

It was her last thought as she hit the button and the lights went out.

19

illie sat silently in the mess hall with the others. After McQuade's short rundown of the *Kurtz* repairs, there didn't seem to be much to say.

They waited to hear Jones's voice over the 'com—or better, to see Ripley walk into the room.

An hour ago, the alert horn had snapped Billie awake and she had run into the corridor, prepared to hear the queen's fury erupting from the lower deck. The alarm had shut off seconds later, and Ana Moto had 'commed shipwide to report that she'd found Ripley unconscious and carried her to medical.

They had all gone to the mess hall to wait it out.

Moto appeared a few minutes later and told

them that the doctor was running a full diagnostic and would call when he knew.

Billie felt so tired that it was all she could do to keep her eyes open. The tension in the room only made her more exhausted. When would it stop? Now it was Ripley who could be dying, the woman she had grown to respect and admire and care about—

Wilks sat beside her and drank coffee. As usual, his expression revealed little. Billie was envious of his control. Nothing seemed to affect him for more than a few seconds; he reacted, then just dealt with what there was.

In comparison, she was a child, chronologically and emotionally. Her inner cries of unfairness were petty and pointless. And they changed nothing. . . .

Billie chewed at her lip and waited.

Wilks toyed with his coffee cup, aware that it was a good time to talk to Billie. He was concerned about Ripley, but Jones was the expert. There was nothing he could do there. Probably not a fuck of a lot he could do here, either.

Billie stared blankly at the table, as if watching a holo. Even when Bueller had been left on Spears's planetoid, she'd been able to talk about it. Sort of.

When Moto and Falk started a conversation across the room, he was ready.

"How are you doing?"

"Fine," she replied, voice dull.

"I'm sorry about Adcox," he said. No answer. "I

wish she were here. I wish I could've traded places with her."

Billie looked at him. "Why? It's not your fault."

"After Ripley left, I was in charge of the APC. I was responsible."

"You didn't make her come here, Wilks! I—" She stumbled on her words, stopped.

Wilks put his hand on her shoulder. "You didn't either," he said.

He felt out of place trying to comfort her, but he couldn't stand the look on her face—it reflected how he felt most of the time. He had learned how to hide it, but it was still there. She hurt. He knew.

She relaxed a little into his hand.

"It's really not your fault, Billie. You didn't make these things."

She looked away for a long time, and finally, she nodded. Her gaze turned to his, her eyes bright with tears, and she nodded again. "No," she said shakily. "I didn't."

Wilks felt his own tight gut loosen a bit. It was a start. Maybe he hadn't fucked up so bad after all—

"Hey, folks," the 'com crackled. "You there?"

It was Jones.

Tully called back. "What is it? How is she?"

Everyone in the room faced the wall 'com. Wilks tightened his hand on Billie's shoulder.

"She's okay," said Jones. "Good as new in no time."

Falk and Moto jumped up, grinning. McQuade

clapped his hand on the edge of his chair and
laughed.

Wilks smiled at Billie, whose entire body relaxed as she started to cry. This crew hardly
knew each other in real time, but Wilks was as relieved as anybody. Ripley was special. Hell, they
were all special. He put his arm around her and
she leaned on him, tears flowing. She would cry
more about this, he understood. There was relief,
and then there was letting go. Not something he
had a lot of practice at himself.

Ripley swam up out of the murk slowly. Someone spoke nearby. She was tired, her head
hurt—

"... now, in no time," said the voice. Far away,
someone laughed. Ripley struggled to open her
eyes.

"What happened?" That voice was distant,
tinny—

The closer voice spoke again. "She sustained a
head injury at some point, probably got hit by the
queen."

Ripley faded out again. Too hard to concentrate.
But then—"queen." Queen. She felt her hands
clench, hard. *Wake up. Wake up*.

"... no cerebrospinal draining, no fracture. I
was worried about hemorrhage, but there's no
signs of that. Mostly fatigue, I think. Mild concus-
sion. She's pretty tough. Tougher than she looks."

Jones. She was on the *Kurtz*, in medlab, and
the queen—

Ripley groaned and rolled her head. She opened her eyes.

Jones stood by a wall 'com. He glanced at her and checked his watch.

"Oops. I have a patient to attend to. I'll let you know when she feels like visitors."

Ripley cringed as she looked around. Cold room, funny smell, shiny instruments. It scared her and she didn't know why.

"Where's the queen?" she said. Her throat was dry.

"Locked up in the containment area. Don't worry. Nothing happened, you just passed out," he said. "Everyone is fine." He got her a glass of water from the dispenser and held her head up so she could drink.

"How long?" she said, lying back.

"About twenty minutes since Moto found you."

Ripley started to sit up. "No offense, Jones, but I don't do doctors. I'd like to go back to my quarters."

"I'd rather you stay here—"

"I'd rather I didn't. I'm fine, right?" She swung her legs over the edge of the table and paused for a moment, head pounding. She had to get *out* of this awful room—

"All right," he said. "But let me help you. You're going to need to be looked at when we get back to Gateway; I don't have any training in your type. I mean, I wouldn't have even *known* without the blood sample."

Ripley stood and pulled away from Jones's outstretched hand.

"What are you talking about? I thought you said I was okay."

"Yeah, you're okay. I'm really impressed, in fact. So close, yet so far apart."

"Jones," she started, exasperated. "What's your point?"

"Don't upset yourself, Ripley. You're fine, but you do need to rest. I just don't understand why you never *told* me. I mean, what if I'd had to do an emergency procedure? Blood transfusion or like that?"

"A-positive," she said. "Don't you have it?"

Jones grinned at her. "Yeah, but you don't. And you don't have RH factors anyway. Although as advanced as you are, I wouldn't be surprised. I'd never have known without the microscope; even the color is perfect. Pretty amazing. Come on, let me help you to your—"

"What the hell *are* you talking about? 'Advanced as I am'?"

"Yeah, I'd heard they were pushing the envelope in the AP labs before the monsters landed, but you are so close it's hard to believe—"

She got it. It was a bad joke. She slapped his hand away, furious. "You're an asshole, Jones! This is not funny. Who the hell do you think you are? Not funny at *all*. Christ!"

His grin melted. "Ripley," he said, eyes wide. "Oh, God. You didn't know? You mean—how could you not know? Shit, I'm sorry—I thought—"

He faltered. His dark features were a mask of embarrassment. Ripley felt her own anger subside a little as she watched the truth on his face. She leaned heavily against the wall.

No, no, it, I—can't be, no, she thought. This is another bad dream, another nightmare. This can't be true. It can't be. I'm human! Not—not—

An android.

20

Wilks opened his door to an exhausted-looking Ripley.

"I know it's late, but can I talk to you for a minute?"

"Yeah, sure. How are you feeling? We thought ..." He trailed off as she brushed past him and sat on the edge of his bed, head down. She ran her hands through her mussed hair. Her shoulders were tense and there were dark smears beneath her eyes. Her face was ashen.

She looked up at Wilks with an expression that he couldn't quite place. Something like—fear? Shame?

"What's going on, Ripley?"

"I know that no one is officially in charge of this thing, but everyone has looked to me this far," she said. She seemed to stare through him, as if she were reciting to a wall.

"That's right," he said carefully. "And you've done a good job."

"Well, I quit. It's yours, Wilks. I want you to finish it."

She stood up as if the conversation was finished and stepped toward the door.

"Hold on a second, Ripley—what's going on here? You just got out of medical, you look like hell, and now you want to drop responsibility for our little stowaway on *me*? How hard did you get knocked on the skull?" He grinned to lighten the tone, but he was surprised.

"It's not open to discussion, Wilks. Look, if you don't want to do it, talk to McQuade, or Moto, or anyone. I don't care. But I'm *out*." Her cheeks were flushed, but Wilks still couldn't pin down the emotion.

"Why?" he said. "Can you tell me that? What happened?"

Ripley dropped her gaze and seemed to shrink. She didn't say anything, but she didn't move to leave, either.

Wilks waited, confused. Since day one this had been Ripley's baby. She'd brought the queen onboard single-handedly, and if it hadn't been for her, he and Billie and Falk would be atomic dust—if the aliens hadn't gotten to them first.

"I just had a long conversation with Jones," she said finally. Her voice was slow and measured and she wouldn't meet his eyes. "I'm a synthetic, Wilks. Fake." She crossed her arms and looked at him, face blank. "I'm not human, and I didn't even know it."

Wilks looked at her for a few beats as it sank in. An android? He took a deep breath. "Are you sure?"

"Jones showed me the blood samples; we ran through the tests. Yeah, I'm sure." She pressed the heel of her hand to her forehead, eyes closed.

"Not to make light of it, Ripley, but so fucking what? You've gotten us this far, and—"

"Don't you *get* it?" Her voice was high and shaky. "Who knows *what* my agenda is—I may have been programmed with this idea by some company that wants a specimen to *study*. What if I'm set up to kill all of you when we get to Earth?" She lowered her voice. "I'm not trustworthy."

"Can you, uh, access your program?"

"No. Apparently I'm too advanced. No mechanicals, no input or export jacks." Her voice was charged with bitter self-disgust. "Jones said he never would have known without a microscan. I can pass for human right down to the microscopic level."

Wilks frowned. "I see your point," he said. "But no shit, I don't think it makes a difference. You could've left us to die back there, you could have killed us already—and who's left on Earth to study anything?" He paused for a moment. "I think wherever your agenda came from, it's a good one. And if the only way to tell is with a microscan, what *is* the difference?"

Ripley walked to the door and pushed it open.

"The difference is me," she said. She stepped into the corridor.

Wilks looked at the half-open door. Jesus and Buddha. How would everyone else take this? Finding out that what they thought was human—

Billie, he thought. Ripley obviously wasn't dealing too well with this. Maybe Billie would have something to say about it; she had loved Bueller even after she had found out the truth. . . .

Wilks went to find her.

Billie knocked at Ripley's door and waited. There was no response. The *Kurtz's* heat had cycled down for the standard night; Billie folded her arms tightly against the chilly air. She knocked again, softer this time.

Maybe she's asleep, she thought. *Good.*

She waited another moment and then walked back to her quarters. Wilks stood up when she stepped into her room.

"She's asleep," said Billie.

"Or just not answering," he said. "Maybe you can talk to her tomorrow."

There didn't seem to be much else to say. He left, went back to his own cubicle. Billie went to hers.

Billie was tired, but there was too much going on to think about sleeping yet. She sat down on the edge of her bed.

What would she have said to Ripley? What *could* she say?

Oh, sorry, Ripley, that's tough. You know, I was in love with a soldier once, and it turned out he wasn't

*real either. I was hurt when I found out—I guess I
felt betrayed. . . .*

That would be very helpful.

Billie exhaled slowly and lay back. She stared
at the ceiling and tried to spot flaws in the smooth
plastic paneling as her mind wandered.

Mitch had been capable of love; she believed
that now. But by the time she had realized it, she
and Wilks had already been on Spears's ship.

Did knowing about Ripley change anything?
Billie thought about the mission so far. From the
start, Ripley had been totally committed to de-
stroying the creatures—no, her respect for Ripley
was solid.

Since Billie had known her, Ripley hadn't
seemed to need anyone. But it sounded like she
could use some support now. In a way, she suddenly seemed *more* real—

More *human*, she thought. The way Mitch had
been in that final transmission.

Billie knew all about the prejudices that people
still held about synthetics; it was hard for some to
talk to machines and feel comfortable.

Was Mitch just a machine? Is Ripley?

After Mitch, she had a different perspective on
things. And this was *about* perspective. Ripley
wasn't born in the usual way, but did that make
her soulless? Or any less valuable as a being?
Where could you draw the line?

Finally Billie slept. She dreamed of questions
with no answers.

• • •

Ripley finally acknowledged her hunger when it became apparent that it wasn't going to go away.

Fine, she thought, *I'm hungry. Big deal.*

It was late morning. She had slept for almost ten hours and had awakened still tired. She lay in bed, eyes closed.

It was all she could think about, and yet there was nothing to think. How *could* she feel? And what did it matter? Her feelings were simulated, false.

At least some things were clearer now. Her lapse of time after the *Sulaco*. The absence of dreams since then. And the intense distrust of doctors—obviously a programmed measure to avoid the truth. Can't let them go poking around in you, they'll figure it out.

The *why* was elusive, and maybe it was pointless besides. All of her beliefs were in question; androids were not to be trusted, they could betray themselves completely. It was their *nature*. The way she had been betrayed ...

The synthetic on the *Nostromo* had been a murderer who had posed as a friend. Bishop had been okay, but—

Ripley frowned. There had even been something about Bishop that was all wrong, some duality, although she couldn't quite remember—

There was a knock at the door.

"Ripley? It's Billie. Can I come in?"

Ripley's heart tightened. *Billie*. The young woman had shown a lot of courage through all of this. Ripley had been proud of her.

Funny, she thought. *How human of me.*

"Not now, Billie."

"It'll only take a minute! Wilks wants to go into deepsleep tonight, and—"

"Go away, Billie. I don't want company." The mere thought of talking about it made Ripley more exhausted.

There was a hesitation. Ripley imagined Billie standing there, searching for magic words: *Nobody cares*, she would say, *really*, *it's okay*—

The idea of Billie pitying her made her feel sick. And the feeling wasn't even real.

Damn.

"Not now."

She heard Billie walk away. She was glad to hear that the others were going into deepsleep; she wanted to be left alone.

Ripley's stomach growled noisily; she pulled her knees to her chest and willed it all to go away.

21

Wilks felt great. He sat up in the chamber and looked around at the cold, sleeping forms of the others. He was surprised at the lack of usual side effects, but only vaguely. What mattered was how he felt.

He pulled on his clothes and grinned at the warm, easy strength in his body. He felt fucking terrific. But it was more than that. There was something—

Absolution, he thought. It was what he had wanted for so long that it had no longer seemed possible. And it didn't seem the slightest bit odd that he had awakened that way; it was about goddamned time. It was like a sense of peace had flowered in him in sleep, a knowledge that everything was finally as it should be. . . .

He laughed out loud as he walked to the stairs. For years he had carried so much, the guilt and torment of the past had weighed so heavy on his shoulders. And for what? It was gone, released into the void of space. There was nothing to wonder at; he was free!

A cool voice spoke gently in his mind, led him through this—revelation. *Freedom*, it said softly, *the key*—

Only one thing left to do. He descended the steps and walked through the APC dock; his feet barely touched the metal. So much of his life wasted! But everything was okay now....

He stepped to the door of the containment chamber and reached for the controls, as if in a dream.

Freedom, life, release—

A flood of warmth and peace washed over him as his hand hovered near the button. The feelings became insistent, stronger.

Let it go, let me go—

Wait. Wilks pulled his hand back, suddenly unsure. What mattered? Where was—

LET ME GO—

A sense of great power and awful dread coursed through him. He staggered back, away from the door. He was an empty space, overwhelmed abruptly with sorrow, despair.

But it was there! his mind screamed. That beautiful calm, that—

Release, freedom—The voice glittered softly with promise. And love.

All he had to do was punch the button.

Wilks crumpled against the wall and wept for the first time since he was a child.

Billie stood in the APC dock. It was cold and the lights were low. She was supposed to meet someone there, but she couldn't recall—

"Billie!"

The muffled voice came through the wall of the containment chamber. The voice that she had known and loved.

"Billie! It's me, Mitch!"

She started toward the door; an inkling of hope welled inside her chest.

"Mitch?" Her voice broke slightly.

"Yeah. Open up, Billie! I love you."

She stopped a few meters away. Her smile faded. No. There was no possible way—

"Billie! Billie, it's Char! Oh, God, don't let it get me, Billie, oh, please, no—"

How could she have thought it was Mitch? Char was in trouble, and Billie was responsible! She ran to the door and reached for the button. But—

Char is dead.

"Don't let it kill me, oh, Billie, don't do this to me, open the door!"

"You're dead," Billie said softly. "You aren't in there." She pulled her trembling hands away from the controls.

"You're right," said the voice on the other side. "And I might as well be dead. You don't give a shit, Billie; it's all about you. Leave me here. None of it matters."

It was Ripley.

"No," said Billie. This was all wrong! "Ripley, I care about you! I want to help, don't you know that? Let me help you—"

Ripley sounded hopeless, lost. "You won't even talk to me, Billie. I thought you were my friend, but, no, you would leave me to die in here—"

"No! I—" Why couldn't she open the door? "Ripley, I can't! There's something in there—"

The queen. The realization hit her full force. She fell back from the door as it all came clear and a chorus of voices called out, begging—

"Let me out—"

"I love you—"

"Please, no—"

Behind it all there was a screaming cry that harmonized with the pleadings of her lost friends. A powerful music, full of now-strident chords, pounding, thundering . . .

It surged over her like a soundful tide and washed everything with gelid darkness. . . .

Ripley sat with her back to the chamber door, the carbine locked and loaded across her lap. The crew had been asleep for two days. She would join them soon, but for now she sat. Waiting . . .

She had spent the first day alternately sleeping and eating. The idea of ending it had surfaced more than once, and she had considered it more carefully each time; who would give a shit about one less android? Just blow herself out of a lock, no great loss. She wasn't necessary to the survival of the plan. The others could get by. . . .

She had been aimlessly looking through the supply hold when the queen had screamed, the sound carrying well in the dead silence of the sleeping *Kurtz*. Ripley had grabbed a rifle almost by reflex and headed for the hold.

She'd run into the APC bay, heart racing wildly, afraid the queen had somehow managed to escape—but everything had been locked up tight. The queen was crying out and hammering at the walls, but she was pent.

The alien mother at her back had been silent for almost an hour now; the tantrum had only lasted a few minutes.

Ripley was glad she was still alive. She had ceased to care about much, but there was still *something*.

The bitch behind me is waiting to die and she is going to take her goddamned children with her when she goes.

Ripley wanted to see that. Had to know that it happened.

Right now, that was enough of a reason for Ripley to live. Whatever she was.

Wilks groaned as light assaulted him. The chamber door fanned open with a hiss and the warmth of his sleep-womb escaped into the cool air. His entire body ached.

He sat up slowly and remembered a great sadness—

The dreams.

"Everybody stay in here," he said. His voice

was a weak croak. He coughed and cleared his throat. "Nobody leaves until we talk!"

The others pulled themselves awake, expressions dazed and sour. Wilks ignored his body's aches as he grabbed his coverall and walked to the door. He dressed quickly in the chill air and waited for the others.

Some part of him relaxed when he saw that Ripley was among them. She had dressed quickly as well, and came to where he stood. She started to step past him.

"Hold on, Ripley. The queen was sending messages while we slept. I think we need to—"

"I don't dream," she said. "Excuse me."

He started to reply and thought better of it. He nodded at her as she stepped by.

Brewster tabbed his shirt and turned toward Wilks, scowling. "What the fuck, Wilks?" he said.

The others looked at him expectantly. He searched their faces for any change, but they all just looked tired and irritable, same as he felt.

"Anybody dream of letting the queen loose?" he said.

"Yes," said Billie.

Ana Moto nodded, as did McQuade and Jones. Brewster's face softened. "Yeah."

"Okay," he said. "We can talk about it over breakfast."

"The message *was* quite powerful," said Moto. "It was like an ongoing advertisement, 'Look what you win if you open the magic door.' It's no wonder you wanted to check with us. You haven't had to deal with it before."

Wilks nodded.

Billie swallowed a bit of soypro and looked at Wilks, curious about what he had dreamed.

"Wanted to make sure none of us were going to play, I suppose," said Brewster.

"Something like that."

"Welcome to the dreamers' club," Moto said.

They sat at one table and ate for the first time in weeks. They would be in range of Gateway in less than twenty hours. Billie's pulse quickened at the thought of Earth. . . .

Ripley had walked by them on their way into the mess hall as she'd carried a tray back to her own room. Billie wished she would have at least eaten with them; that there were three fewer crew members was bad enough, but Ripley was *alive*.

"Hey, where's the boss?" said Brewster. "Why isn't she eating with us?"

"Yeah," Tully added. "We need to go over what we're going to do to get past Gateway."

Billie glanced over at Wilks. He laid down his fork.

"Ripley is having some personal problems," Billie said.

"What kind of personal problems?" Falk asked.

Wilks nodded at Billie to continue. She stood. Everyone stopped eating and looked at her.

"We need to talk about that," she began. "I'm not sure—Ripley would probably rather not discuss it, but she would want you all to know." She sounded much calmer than she felt.

"Ripley is an artificial person. An android. She apparently didn't find out until the medical check she just had, and the news has affected her badly."

She stopped and looked around the table. The room was uncomfortably silent.

"Ripley has asked if I would take over where she left off," said Wilks. "But it's going to have to be a combined effort. I'm not really the leader type, and—"

"How the fuck could she not *know*?" said McQuade. "Don't they all know what they are?"

"Not necessarily," said Jones. "Ripley didn't."

"We trusted her," said Tully quietly.

Billie felt a spark of anger.

"That explains how she managed the queen by herself," said Falk. He sounded depressed.

"If I had known," started McQuade, "I wouldn't—"

"If you had known, *shit*," Billie said. She remained standing; the cool dining hall had suddenly gotten very warm. "Ripley didn't *know*, do you get that?" She glared at Tully. "She trusted *herself*! How would you feel? Do you think she did this on *purpose*?"

She turned to Falk. "The last thing she needs is bigotry from this crew!"

She was losing it. Billie took a deep breath and forced herself to sit down. "Jones is better qualified to answer questions about it—"

"Not really," said Jones. "All I can tell you is that she's as close to human as I've ever seen.

And I think Billie is right. Ripley's a good leader."
He stopped and looked vaguely embarrassed.

The others absorbed the information.

Moto nodded slowly.

"Okay," said Wilks. "The more important issue
here is that we're getting closer to the station. I
think that there are a few people there who would
like to have a little chat with us. . . ."

As Wilks discussed some possibilities, Billie
calmed herself. Tully and Falk both looked at her
in ways she thought were apologetic, although
McQuade still seemed pissed off.

She was surprised at herself, but not as much
as she would have thought, even a few months before. The outburst had felt good, and she thought
it might even have helped. Ripley hadn't done
anything *wrong*. It was distressing that any of
these people could overlook her strengths.

Billie yearned for the kind of courage that
Ripley possessed. She would need it to help Amy
. . . if Amy was still alive.

She refocused on the discussion, heart pounding.

22

Wilks sat in control with McQuade and Tully. In theory, the ship ought to be out of Gateway's visual and sensor range. Never knew but some technogeek with a telescope might be looking right at them, but that wasn't likely.

Wilks gripped the back of Tully's chair tightly and hoped that their shielded call would go through.

"Now we wait," said Tully as she finished tapping the keys. "If we're lucky, she'll catch her messages soon."

"And if she doesn't?" said McQuade.

"We wait longer," Wilks said. A coded direct signal could be channeled accurately if you knew what you were doing. In theory, outsiders wouldn't be able to collect it unless they were looking very carefully, and even then, they wouldn't be able to tap into it. There was some risk, but it ought to be minimal, and it was one they had to take.

Time passed.

A burst of static crackled over the 'com, a hum as compressed voxfiles expanded. And there was the time delay, but—

"About goddamn time. I expected you a week ago."

Tully smiled. "Hey there, Fem Elliot! How's life in the box?"

Once again the radio waves took their sweet and slow time and they waited for the reply.

"Maria? I should've known you'd still be around! Say, you reckon you got enough scramble on this signal? It's taking a hell of a lot of my comp's memory. The officials here aren't *that* smart, you know. Just how important do you think you are?"

Wilks leaned toward the 'com. "Thought we'd check in and see what *you* think."

"Ooh, my heart! Is that the infamous Sergeant Wilks? How's the action, Sarge?"

"Not bad, Leslie. We got what we were looking for."

"That's great, folks! Congratulations. And how is everyone?"

Wilks said, "We've had a few losses."

There was a longer pause than the waves needed. "I'm sorry to hear that."

"Yeah," said Wilks.

Tully spoke up. "Our immediate concern is who *else* has been expecting us. Whatcha got, Les?"

"Well. Y'all raised quite a fuss a few months back. I believe the terms were 'subversive' and 'mentally unstable.' Oh, and 'malicious intent.' To make a long story short, the official trickle-down was that a bunch of nuts stole a ship for no good reason except to fuck with the powers-that-be."

McQuade chuckled. "Not too far off," he said.

Wilks frowned. "Is that all?"

"You're kidding, right? *Unofficially*, General Peters got a very large boot jammed in his very tight ass for not recognizing the magnitude of your insanity. There are warrants out for all of you. The good news is that they think you're crackpots so maybe you'll get stuck in a nice clean hospital room and not a regular cell. And they're not expecting you for another six weeks, if then."

"Why's that?" said Wilks.

"Oh, they turned up a map in your quarters that placed your destination much farther away," she said.

Billie stepped forward, her pale face tensed and eager. Wilks hadn't even noticed her come in.

"Leslie, it's Billie. How are things on Earth?"

"Communication's been shot for weeks. Atmospheric static, sunspots acting up, something like that. But whatever the bugs are doing down there, it's gotten worse."

"What about the satellite uplinks?" said Billie.

She looked close to tears, but her voice was strong.

"The last signals we got are old news—and I have to tell you, it wasn't good. Anyone left on Earth probably belongs to the aliens now, one way or the other. I'm sorry."

Wilks put his hand on Billie's shoulder, but she shook it off. "Listen. Do me a favor and pipe the last few days of transmissions to us. Can you do that?"

"No problem."

"Thank you," Billie said. She walked out of the room.

"Listen, I'm glad to hear from you, but let's go easy with this. Even with the scramble—I'll let you know if anything important comes up. And take care, okay?"

"You too," Wilks said.

The 'com went silent. McQuade turned to Wilks. "Doesn't sound like we're going to win any votes here," he said.

Wilks shrugged. "To get to the bombs we're going to be in their gun sights at some point," he said. "And we've got the queen. I doubt we'll get any help from them, but maybe we can persuade them to let us have our shot. And even at worst case, they won't blow us out of space—they want the *Kurtz* back."

McQuade nodded, but looked uncertain. Wilks walked back to talk to the rest of the crew. The station wouldn't spot them for a few more hours, so they still had time to come up with alternate plans.

Wilks knew that he was good in tight situations; he was trained for it. But shit like this—

Dammit, why isn't Ripley doing this? Fuck her humanity, or lack of it—they were better off with her in charge. He knew his limits, and they were not far off.

Billie sat alone in the medlab at the small computer. The room was cold and gleaming white; it gave her a strange kind of nostalgia for the hospitals she had spent most of her life in. Right now there were more important things on her mind, however. . . .

She tapped in a short description of Amy and waited for a match.

The screen flickered. A fuzzy picture flashed onscreen of a young girl with a bad haircut. She stared at Billie for a few seconds, eyes too serious for a child. How old was she now? Thirteen? Fourteen maybe?

Oh, baby, thought Billie. Her heart tightened, but at the same time she felt a huge relief.

"Is it on?" Amy said. Her voice had deepened slightly, and it looked as if she had made an effort to wipe her face clean.

"Go ahead, honey," said a voice offscreen.

"Me and Daddy are in a factory that used to make microchips in Northern California. We're probably going to move soon. Uncle Paul is gone now. He went to look for food almost two weeks ago and I hope that he is just hiding, but we don't think so." Her face clouded as she spoke, but her young eyes didn't waver from the camera.

"It's getting warmer all the time. We have a new friend named Mordecai, and he says that he thinks the aliens have heated things up somehow with their nesting materials."

She smirked, a surprisingly adult gesture. "Mordecai also says that the goddamn religious fucks are as bad as the aliens now." She glanced past the camera sheepishly and then raised her eyebrows, obviously the recipient of a nasty look.

"Well, *he* said it!"

A sigh offscreen. "I know, honey. Go on."

"Anyway. We wanted to tell you that the aliens have been acting strange for a few weeks. They have been grouping together and staying quiet for days at a time, and no one knows why."

The little girl frowned. "I guess that's all," she said.

The old man's voice stated the date and coordinates as usual and the screen blanked.

Billie stared into the empty monitor for another moment and then laughed abruptly. She was still alive! The transmission was over a month old, but the family had survived for so long already that she *had* to be.

I would know if she was dead, she thought. *I would know.*

The connection that Billie felt was too intense for it to be otherwise. The coordinates listed were already etched into her mind.

Orona's bombs were part of an old-style military arsenal located in a remote area of the northwestern United States. Billie had been there once, when she and Wilks had escaped from Earth and ended up at Spears's planetoid. She and Wilks and Mitch . . .

She shook the memory. Surely a military bunker would have some kind of transportation . . . ?

It wasn't impossible. Everything was falling into place; she was *meant* to save that family. To save Amy.

Billie felt fully awake for the first time since leaving the mother alien's planet. She had been a follower for a long time, had taken directions most of her life. This was her chance to make a difference. And it wasn't some distant dream anymore, it was *here*. Not on the scale of total extermination of the aliens—but it was hers, it was taking a stand that mattered most.

She sat and daydreamed of possible futures. Hang on, Amy. Just a little bit longer.

"This is Gateway Station calling. Please identify yourself."

Wilks looked at McQuade and nodded.

"This is Captain McQuade of the *Kurtz*," he said. "I would like to speak with your CO."

The time lag stretched past its limit. Wilks imagined the flurry of activity they had just caused and almost smiled.

"Bet we got some people pissing in their drawers right now," said McQuade.

"Sir," said a voice, "please stand by for Major Stone."

"Here we go," Wilks said.

"Captain McQuade, this is Major Stone." The

major's voice rang with authority. "Open your control modem for override."

"Actually, Major, we just wanted to talk for a minute. We have—"

"Captain, we'll be glad to talk to you when you get here. You know procedure. Now if you'll just let us help you arrive safely, I'm sure we can work this out." Major Stone spoke slowly and carefully, as if he was directing a child. Or a mental case.

"Major Stone, this is Sergeant Wilks. We *are not* coming to Gateway. We have the queen alien onboard the *Kurtz* and we're taking her to Earth. There is no need for Gateway military involvement; this is just to let you know." He attempted to sound calm and reasonable.

The major did not bite. "Sergeant, we are already sending people to fetch you. Now, you can come in like civilized men or we can drag you in kicking and screaming, but you *are* coming to this station! Do you copy?"

Wilks silenced the 'com. "Tully?"

"Station dispatched a ship," she said. "I got the drive signal spewing all over my long-range sensor array."

"Well, we gave it a shot. Okay, McQuade, get us out of here." He hit the 'com button and spoke quickly. "Gotta go, Major, nice talking to you."

"Wilks, you can't—"

He cut Stone off and switched on the shipwide. "Heads up, people. Looks like Gateway is coming to dinner and we don't have a lot of time. The shit is about to hit the fan."

•   •   •

Wilks's message echoed through the empty APC bay. Ripley ignored it. They would figure something out; it didn't matter as long as she still had the queen.

"Wouldn't want to miss the reunion," she whispered. "I gotta take you home to die with your babies, monster. *Every*body dies."

Nothing else mattered.

23

"Can we outrun it?" said Falk.

"No," Brewster said. "That ship is more maneuverable and a lot faster."

"They won't fire at us, will they?" That from Jones.

"I don't think so," said Wilks. "They want us back in one piece. Well, at least they want the *ship* back in one piece. Same difference, far as we're concerned."

The crew stood in the dining hall nervously. They had about an hour before Gateway's ship would be in range. Billie noticed that for a change it was too warm. She wiped at her face and wondered where Ripley was.

Tully answered Jones: "They *could* try a gun or

laser-shot at our drives to damage us enough so we couldn't fly straight. But that's iffy—they might miss and punch a hole in us, accidentally destroy something they can't fix real easy. Or cheap. I'm with Wilks; I don't think they'll risk that."

"So what can they do?" said Jones. "Fly circles around us until we get dizzy and surrender?"

No one laughed.

Tully said, "They can disable the *Kurtz*'s control systems with an electromagnetic pulse and tow us in. That'd be the easiest—just get within range and push a button. That's what I would do."

"Our electronics aren't hardened?" said Falk.

"On this rust bucket? Sheeit."

Billie frowned. "Can't we do it to them first?"

"EMP capabilities in a *freighter*?" said Brewster. "Dream on. This ship isn't designed for combat of any kind. No shields, no weapons—basically, we're screwed."

But what about Amy? Billie wanted to shout. They couldn't just *quit*—

Moto sighed. "They won't *kill* us back on Gateway. I mean, once we get there, we could explain things. We do have the queen. The military could take her and finish the job for us—probably badly, but at least it'd get done."

No one replied and Billie watched acceptance start to settle on their faces. They might not like it, but what choice did they have?

It's not fair, she thought, and wiped at her brow again, frustrated. That after all of this, after people had *died* to make this work, they were just going to roll over and—

Suddenly, there was a grin on her face. Something Tully had said triggered it. "Wait. There's a way," she said. "I have an idea."

They all stared at her.

Engines idle, the *Kurtz* coasted toward Earth through the blackness, falling into the gravity well in a spiral that, if not interrupted, would end with whatever charred remains survived the reentry burn splashing down in the Indian Ocean.

"Everything is powered down," said Tully, "except lights and communications." Her voice sounded tinny over the headset, even though engineering was directly below them.

"Moto? Got your set on?" said Wilks.

"Yeah. Ready."

Wilks and McQuade waited for the call in the control room. The others would be strapped in behind them, in the crew area. Wilks hadn't spoken to Ripley, but had explained the plan over the shipwide; he hoped she had listened.

"*Kurtz* crew please acknowledge. This is Commander Hsu of the *Adams*."

"This is McQuade," the captain growled. "What the fuck do you want? I'm busy here."

"Sir," said Hsu politely, "we're here to escort you back to Gateway. There is no need to be unreasonable. Open your modem and we can avoid any unpleasantness—"

McQuade cut in. "No way. We're going to Earth and there's nothing you can do about it, Hsu.

Your weapons won't work on us—we're blessed! You can't stop us! We're invulnerable!"

On his last words, the lights flickered and went out.

A few seconds passed and the mechanical emergency backups switched on.

They'd been EMPed. If their systems had been running, half of the electronics would have probably been fried.

Wilks turned to McQuade. "Well, my guess is that you are now more or less officially crazy, Captain. Hsu probably has the med team on Gateway standing by with a full case of Trinomine patches by now; you'll get doubles."

Wilks tapped his headset back to life. "Moto, Tully. Let's get going."

It didn't take long. Twenty minutes or so. Then, a dull thunk echoed through the ship and the *Kurtz* slowed, finally stopped. After a moment, the ship began to move in a new direction, toward Gateway, though they couldn't see that from inside with all the systems off-line.

"They got their magnetic tow cable in place," Wilks said almost under his breath, as if those in the other ship might somehow hear him.

McQuade nodded. "Fish on a line."

If this doesn't work, thought Wilks, *we're going to be in* really *deep shit.*

Billie sat in the crew area with Jones, Falk, and Brewster. Falk had laughed quietly at McQuade's speech, which had carried to them through the partition. They all waited silently now, tense.

Brewster unbuckled his strap and moved to the chair next to Billie's.

"Okay if I sit here?" he said.

She nodded and watched as he strapped back in and then turned to her. He seemed unsure of himself.

"How are you doing?" he said.

"I'm okay. I had a rough time for a while, but it's gotten better." She was glad that she meant what she said.

"Good to hear," he said. "I've been coming to terms with some of my own shit." He paused, obviously wanting to say more.

Billie smiled gently at him. "Dylan. We both have had a lot to deal with on this trip, and there's still a ways to go. But I consider us friends and I want you to know that no matter what happens, I wish you well."

"I don't regret it," he said quietly. Even in the dimly lit room, she could see that he had reddened slightly. He touched her hand.

"Neither do I." Their night together had been nice. She held his fingers in her own for a moment and squeezed lightly before letting go.

There were bigger things to be dealing with than a sexual encounter between them, and she felt like this was his acknowledgment of that; Dylan was okay. And so was she. More or less.

"Get ready," Wilks called back to them.

Billie leaned back in her seat and closed her eyes.

● ● ●

"Ready." Tully's voice crackled in Wilks's ears. He nodded at McQuade and held up his hand. The captain leaned to the controls and watched for the signal.

Billie's plan was almost embarrassingly simple. Play dead until they were being towed and then scoot forward and tap the other ship's drive control surfaces hard enough to damage them. By the time Gateway sent another ship, the *Kurtz* would be well on its way to Earth. What the hell, it was just goofy enough to have a chance.

"Stand by," Wilks called over his shoulder.

He pointed at McQuade. "Go!"

The *Kurtz* hummed back to life. McQuade hit the controls and the ship rocketed forward and to one side.

For an impossibly long time they hurtled through space. Wilks gritted his teeth.

The body of the ship shuddered with the impact, a loud crash. Even braced as he was, it jarred Wilks, hard. Then they were moving again, aslant to the ship they'd just hit.

The magnetic line snapped taut and the coupler was peeled off as the smaller ship was knocked away by the collision.

There goes the insurance, Wilks thought. He remembered an old joke about whiplash. *No time to dick around, now, Wilks.* "Shut it down *fast!*" he ordered.

The *Adams* could still trigger another pulse—

The system went dead; Tully and Moto had pulled everything off-line again. He hoped.

Wilks mentally counted to ten and then spoke into the set.

"Did they get us?"

"Nope," said Tully. She sounded out of breath.

"Hook up perimeter sensors," said Wilks. A few of the console lights blinked on. McQuade scanned the small screen and then laughed.

They were coasting, but moving at a good clip. Time passed, seemed to Wilks like a long chunk of it.

"Out of effective range," McQuade said. "And it looks like they're flying in circles."

Wilks grinned. "Good work down there," he said to engineering. "Get us back online."

"You know what to do, Captain," he said to McQuade.

As the *Kurtz* relit her systems, coming back to life, Wilks tapped the shipwide 'com. "Congratulations, Billie. Looks like we're going to Earth."

Ripley sat in her room alone. She wasn't particularly surprised that they were still on their way; the people onboard weren't stupid. Wilks had apparently turned into quite the leader—

Someone knocked at her door.

"Ripley? You home? It's Billie."

She considered not answering and then sighed. The *Kurtz* wasn't that big; where else could she be?

"Come back later," she said.

"No. I need to talk to you now."

Ripley sighed again. *May as well get it over with.* "Come in."

Billie walked in and sat on the edge of the bed. "How's it going?"

She looked different to Ripley somehow. Not as shy, perhaps, more self-assured. She had always thought of Billie as nervous in confrontative situations, but the young woman sitting on her bed looked anything but.

"How's it going? Why, everything's great. Wonderful. Couldn't be better."

"Really? I've gotten the impression that you don't like us much anymore."

Ripley raised her eyebrows. "Don't play games, Billie."

The younger woman shrugged. "Why not? You are."

Ripley was irritated. "This is what you needed to discuss with me? This is my business, you know, and—"

"—and you don't have to explain yourself to anyone. By all means, Ripley, don't worry about rationalizing on *my* account. But this excursion was *your* idea, and now you're leaving us hanging."

Ripley didn't respond. *So what?* she thought angrily. *You had your reasons for coming along.* Obviously she just wanted to bitch; fine. And she was right—Ripley didn't have to explain it.

"We need you, Ripley. I need you. You're important to me." She took a deep breath.

Here it comes, thought Ripley.

"I admire you," said Billie. "I guess that's what I needed to say. I wish that I had your strength in a lot of ways."

"Don't you mean that past tense?" said Ripley. She realized she sounded bitter, but who the fuck was Billie to come in and dump this on her? "It's not *me*, Billie! You admire a program, a machine."

Billie looked at her unwaveringly. "I was in love with a machine once," she said. Her voice softened. "His name was Mitch. Are you telling me that my love had no value because of what he was? That his love for me was some kind of trick, a—a glitch?"

Ripley turned away from Billie's gaze. This was not the pity she had expected.

"I'm not Mitch," she said.

"No," said Billie. "You're Ripley. I saw your broadcasts long before we ever met; I heard the stories. You act just like that Ellen did, far as I can tell. So what if you're an artificial person? My guess is that whoever made you used who you *were* to do it. So, you're a copy of yourself. So maybe you aren't perfect. So, who the fuck is? If you want to sit there and feel sorry for yourself because you aren't the woman you thought you were, go ahead. It won't change anything. And if we fuck this up because you won't help, you can blame that on yourself, too."

Billie stood, stared at her for a moment, then walked out without speaking again.

Ripley stared after her. Jesus.

Jesus.

24

They made it to Earth with no more trouble from Gateway.

That's something, at least, thought Wilks. They had achieved atmosphere without a hitch and now flew high over an ocean toward the North American continent. Brewster was at the controls; he was a better pilot in air than McQuade.

"ETA approximately ninety minutes," he said.

"Okay," said Wilks. He unstrapped from the co-pilot's chair and walked toward the dining hall. The others would be there in a few minutes. He moved slowly, lost in thought.

What next? They had made it to Earth with a psychic alien queen to—they hoped—obliterate the infestation there; they had lost three people, and their leader had developed an aversion to leading. Every bug on the planet would be after their asses once they set down. Aside from the fact that even if they succeeded at this point, going back to Gateway probably meant brainwipes and locktime as a reward.

Wilks grinned as he stepped out of the corridor. *All of that and the food's great, too*, he thought.

"What's so funny, Wilks?"

Ripley stood at a dispenser, a cup of coffee in hand. The room was empty except for the two of them.

"I was just thinking of all the fun we've been having so far," he said. "Hello, Ripley." He acted casual, but it was good to see her. He went to another dispenser and ordered a steak. Well, what passed for steak. The joy of soy.

Something that looked like a steaming, squashed-flat turd arrived. Wilks shook his head and picked up the tray.

Ripley walked with him to a table and sat across from him.

"Wilks," she began, "I want to thank you for stepping in to run this operation. And now that we're here, I'd like to offer my help—unless you've got everything under control. . . ." The last was almost a question.

He poked at the cutlet on his tray. "Actually, I was hoping you'd say something like that," he said. "Welcome back. I'm a crappy leader."

"Sounds like you've been doing fine," she said. He shrugged. "What changed your mind?"

"Something Billie said. It pissed me off enough to start thinking about how I've been dealing with things." She stared at her hands for a minute and then looked up at him.

"Whatever my circumstances are, we still have a job to do, right?" She smiled, but there was no humor in the expression.

Falk and Moto walked into the room together, chatting. They stopped when they saw who was there.

"Hey, good to see you, Ripley," Moto said.

Falk grinned at her. "Yeah, you gonna stop Wilks from looking like an asshole?"

"I'll do my best," she said. "Miracles are difficult, you know?"

Wilks laughed. He felt better than he had since deepsleep.

Billie arrived. She waved to them and went to a dispenser for coffee. Wilks watched her smile brighten at the sight of Ripley, and felt a rush of warmth for her. She had changed so much since he'd broken her out of the hospital on Earth; she was stronger, braver, more beautiful—

Instead of immediately stifling the thought as he had in the past, he let it sit for a moment. Billie didn't need him to protect her anymore. She had demonstrated many times that she was more than capable of standing on her own. He felt comfortable working with her, he trusted her—she was really the closest thing he had to a friend. But a lover?

Why the fuck not? You're only old enough to be her father and you've got enough emotional trouble for two—bet she'd jump at the chance!

"You awake, Wilks?"

Billie waved a hand in front of him before she sat down. He blinked. Everyone was there now except the pilot.

. . . good time to daydream, Sarge, maybe you'd like to recite some fucking poetry to yourself while the crew takes care of things—

"Sorry," he said, and smiled at her. "Just thinking."

He suddenly recalled one of the sayings from boot camp that he hadn't thought of in decades: Don't be a fool for your tool.

He shook his head and put all those thoughts aside. Later.

"So how are we going to unload our cargo without getting eaten by it?" said Moto.

"Or getting our butts kicked by her unhappy children?" said McQuade.

Although the questions weren't necessarily directed at her, Ripley felt that they were waiting for her response.

"I've got a pretty good idea of the layout on where we're headed," she said. "We're going to have to do this quick; she'll be calling the creatures to her before we even land."

Billie broke in. "She's calling them already, I think. I watched some of the 'casts that Leslie sent over from about six weeks ago—the people on Earth said that the aliens have been gathering together and not attacking as often."

"Perhaps corresponding with when we abducted the mother," finished Moto. "Sounds like they're getting ready."

The crew watched Ripley, waited for her to speak. She was vaguely surprised that she had been accepted back with no confrontations, but didn't want to dwell on it. Her own problems were not a priority right now.

"This is going to be tight," she said. "The arsenal is set into the side of a mountain—we drop the queen on the other side and work fast enough to be done before the majority of her brood shows up. They might know about where she's landing, but not exactly."

"Not that it's important or anything, but does anyone know how to set up the bombs?" said Falk.

Ripley sighed. Sooner or later it was going to come up. "It's in my program," she said. She felt resigned as she looked at each of their faces and wondered what she would see. No one spoke for a moment.

Tully smiled. "Well, thank-fucking-Buddha," she said brightly. "That's something."

"Do you think the bunker will have been raided?" That from Jones.

Wilks shrugged. "Maybe. I'd say definitely, but it's an isolated area."

The whole topic had been glossed over as quickly as it had come up. Ripley suddenly realized that she wasn't going to get the response she had expected. For however the crew members felt about it, they seemed to have come to terms with her as a synthetic—at least on a working level.

Great, she thought, *if I don't glitch it and kill them all.*

Brewster's voice came over the 'com. "Hey, ya'll might want to come check this out—we're over land now. Looks like someone had a pretty wild party last night and wrecked the place." His attempt to sound casual was strained.

Several of them looked at Ripley. She nodded.

"We have as much of a plan as we're going to get," she said. "Let's go see what there is."

As Ripley followed the others into the corridor, Billie lagged back and put her hand on Ripley's arm. They walked slowly behind the others.

"Listen, what about Amy?" said Billie.

Ripley frowned. "The girl from the 'casts?"

Billie nodded. "We have to help her. She's not far from the site, an hour or two maybe, and I could take a flier to go get her."

"How do you know she's alive?"

"She is. I know." Billie looked anxious, her face tight.

Ripley remembered how important the girl had been to Billie back on the station. She stopped walking and faced the young woman. On the one hand, she knew exactly how she felt; on the other hand, there were bigger goals here.

"Billie," she said gently, "we can look at the situation when we get there, but we're not going to have much time. Whether she's alive or not, I don't know if we can afford to do it. I'm sorry."

For a second, a look of panic and frustration flashed across Billie's face, so intense that Ripley thought the girl would scream. Then she relaxed and dropped her gaze to the floor.

"I hear you," she said. She ran one hand

through her long hair. "But I won't give it up without trying." She looked up at Ripley, expression set.

"Well. We'll see what we can do."

Billie walked ahead of her, head still down. Ripley felt sorry for her, but they all had their own shit to work through. The important thing, the *only* thing, was their mission.

Billie stood with her arms crossed and watched Earth tell her story. The *Kurtz* flew high over the eastern states, too high to see unaided most of the destruction that the cameras fed to the ship's magnification screen. The men and women around her stood silently, their faces expressionless as they took in the ruins of the mother planet.

The midday sun spared nothing. The screen showed an overview of a dead city. Here, several blocks of burnt and crumbled buildings that had once towered. Filth littered the streets, parts of cars, vague splotches of blackness and greasy shadow that united the wreckage into a grim tapestry. Everywhere were exploded bits of plastecrete and wood, random pieces of melted metal and brick and bone.

The screen switched, cut to another shot. It was like the picture before, and the picture before that—ravaged and lifeless. This was an industrial area, a series of long, low buildings ripped apart. Billie could see where someone had tried to barricade one—huge crosses of some material covered one wall, right next to a giant hole through the building. An explosion, perhaps ...

Cut to a row of identical houses, windows smashed and doors open or gone. There was life here; Billie realized with disgust that the slight movement around the houses could only be an army of vermin.

The *Kurtz* grabbed random pictures of towns and cities and parks that were lost to humanity. The crew seemed stunned; there were no wisecracks, none of the usual banter that Billie had come to expect from the soldiers. She had grown up in hospitals, hadn't been a part of this world—but the thought that it had simply ceased to exist ...

Billie widened her eyes at the next shot.

"Hey," said Brewster excitedly. "Is that—" He shut up abruptly. There was a small group of people moving down a road. At first glance Billie had felt great hope—until she realized that the four or five figures were dragging another one in lengths of chains. The group stumbled along, tattered, holding weapons—they seemed to look up at the sky, at the ship. Billie remembered the vid she had seen back at the station, the human sacrifice—here were the fanatics, hunting for people to act as incubators. The last insane remnants of humanity.

She thought of what Ripley had said—not enough time to see about Amy—and felt her resolve strengthen. She would help Amy and her family or die trying, time or not. Fuck it.

Billie broke away from the screen and looked

around. The others all seemed lost in worlds of their own. She noticed that Moto and Falk had linked hands. Billie almost smiled at the small reminder that there were still good things. Not many, but some.

She noticed that Wilks's gaze also rested on Falk's and Moto's interlaced fingers. He looked up at her and smiled briefly, sadness heavy on his scarred face. She was surprised that he had let an emotion slip past his normally unshakable facade. As he looked away, she felt a strong urge to comfort him; Billie had never really thought about it before, but it occurred to her now that Wilks was very important to her.

David, she thought. The name sounded strange in her head, but then he was a strange man; so strong, yet so emotionally uncertain—

Billie turned back to the monitor. What was important was that they were here; one way or another, everything was building, coming to a head. . . .

From the hold, the unmistakable cries of the captive queen filtered out. She screamed and pounded in her chamber high over the silent Earth as they headed toward whatever fate held, almost as if she knew what her own end was to be.

If she did, she was ahead of them.

25

As if on cue, the on-screen pictures came to life. The queen howled uselessly and down on Earth, dark, loping figures began to appear. Only a few at first, but the numbers quickly increased. Each shot showed dozens of the creatures as they ran in one direction—after the path of the *Kurtz*.

Ripley felt a rush of cold triumph edged with worry. This was what she had expected, the beginning of the end, but if they fucked up now—

"Holy shit," said McQuade. "Looks like we got a riot coming up."

The monitor showed hundreds of the aliens as they raced through the blackened remains of some large city. Even as they watched, handfuls of the shiny insectile shapes erupted from the wreckage to join the advancing group.

"We'll never make it," Tully said. "There's too many."

Ripley glanced at the woman sharply. Tully didn't look so good—eyes wide, taking short breaths.

"*Tully.* We're headed toward a very isolated area, surrounded by mountains and water. It's going to take them longer than us to get there by land."

The hacker took a deep breath and then nodded at Ripley. "I—yeah, I hear you."

"Good. Start digging for topography maps, anything useful on Northern California and Oregon. Look at adjacent land as well. Go use medlab, okay?"

Tully nodded again and then stood. Having a job to do helped, Ripley knew. The woman looked more collected as she walked past the others.

Dr. Jones smiled at Ripley and then followed Tully.

"Brewster, how long we got?"

"Thirty minutes, give or take."

"Fine. Moto, why don't you and I go see what we can scrounge in the way of tools."

Moto let go of Falk's hand and went to the stairwell.

Captain McQuade sat down in the copilot's chair. "Guess I'll make sure Brewster doesn't crash us," he said.

"That leaves weapons detail to us," said Wilks. "Billie? Falk?"

Ripley nodded. Good. Seeing the planet's condition had been bad, but they all had something to do to keep the images of death at bay for a while. It would all be over before long.

"Tell Tully to call me as soon as she gets a fix on geography," she said. She directed this at Brewster as she followed Moto down the ladder.

The queen screamed in the hold below, sent her message to the Earth's breed.

Ripley grinned tightly as she took the steps. The bitch would have plenty to scream about soon enough.

Wilks watched the mountains grow as the *Kurtz* got closer to its destination. They had all regrouped around the control area and waited now while Brewster efficiently maneuvered the ship through the forested landscape. Thankfully, the monitor revealed less destruction out here.

The mother alien still beat at the walls downstairs, but there was no sign of her children through the blanket of trees. Yet.

There were several small peaks, all part of a range that ran through the Northwest. According to Tully's read, a few of them were volcanic, although none were currently active.

That'd be a kick, he thought, *we land and get buried in lava*.

They would drop the queen in a small, enclosed valley near the base of Orona's mountain and then fly to the arsenal a few minutes farther west. Since most of the creatures would come from inland, this would save the *Kurtz* from being trampled by them on their way to the queen; or so Wilks hoped.

The ship moved slowly over the treetops toward a towering mountain.

"We got a hole," said Tully quickly. "A big one." She listed the coordinates to Brewster.

Wilks grinned at Ripley. The queen might not take off running if they could find a cave to dump her into. There was no way to be sure, but Wilks had never seen one of the creatures traipse around in the open if there was somewhere dark to hide. They could only hope that the mother was similar to the other queens in that regard. When Ripley had mentioned the idea, he had once again been very glad that she was back in charge.

"Great," said McQuade. "That thing is starting to get on my nerves."

"Amen," said Falk.

The ship moved at a crawl. Wilks spotted the cavern, a dark opening in the rocks at ground level.

Perfect. He was ready. As soon as they dumped the alien, they would hurry to the bunker and get to work. Unless the setup was completely destroyed, they could fix it fast and get the fuck off the planet. It was probably just a rewire job—

"Ready, kids?" said Brewster. The *Kurtz* was in place.

"Do it," said Ripley.

They all watched Brewster push the button to open the outer hatch. A faint hum from the console, and a small red light flashed.

"*Shit*," said Ripley.

The hatch hadn't opened. The queen continued to scream.

"What the fuck is wrong?" said Wilks.

"I don't—mechanical failure somewhere," said Brewster. He touched the button again. The light blinked.

"EMP?" said Billie.

"No, we got off-line in time, I'm sure of it," said Moto.

Wilks looked over at Ripley. She chewed at her lip for a second and then slapped her hand against the console.

"She's pressing on the goddamn door!" said Ripley. "Stupid bitch is probably punching the pretty button, blocking her own goddamn exit."

She turned to the stairwell. "Open shipwide 'com and try it again when I say so, Brewster. Wilks, come with me."

He followed Ripley down the stairs. The roar of the engines was incredibly loud as they hurried through the APC bay together.

"The door from here is sealed!" he shouted to her. Ripley ignored him and jogged over to a tool cabinet set into the wall. She tossed a spanner to him and grabbed a second wrench, stepped to the wall and hit it. Wilks joined her, began to beat at the alloy with the spanner.

"Hey, asshole, over here!" Ripley shouted. "Come on, come *on*!"

Wilks hit the wall high, again and again. Between the engines, the queen, and the echoing crash of metal on metal, he was surprised that he heard the new sounds. Through the wall came an awful scraping noise, nails on kleersteel. Or rather, talons on alloy.

Ripley hit the door once more and then shouted to the 'com behind her. "Go!"

A few seconds passed, and the ship suddenly lifted slightly as the queen's cries faded to nothing. Wilks turned to face Ripley. She was still looking at the containment chamber.

"Not that smart, is she?" she said. She spoke loudly to be heard over the engines.

As they headed back upstairs, Wilks rephrased to himself an earlier thought; he was fucking *thrilled* that Ripley was back in charge.

The ship sped to the far side of the mountain in the early afternoon. Even as tense as she was, Billie felt some pleasure as she looked at the environment. It occurred to her that she had seen very little natural beauty in her life. She had grown up in cold, desolate places, had only seen green trees on holovids or in biolabs. Here were thousands, they covered the mountainous area in shades of emerald. All of it a waste ...

They skimmed another small peak and Billie saw the bunkers. The land was flat, wide enough to land two ships the size of the *Kurtz*, the trees cleared away. Directly ahead of them was a low hill, perhaps a tenth the height of the ice-capped mountain where they had left the queen. There were several buildings grouped around it, short and ugly blocks of plastecrete arranged in a semi-circle. A huge metal gate was set into the hill with yellow lines painted across it; the middle of the door had been blown apart.

Billie felt her breath catch in her throat when she spotted them, half hidden—two small fliers and an APC sat in between two of the buildings.

"It's dead," said Tully. "No activity on the sensors."

"Let's bring her in," said Ripley. "Keep an eye on the readings—it may not be as easy as it looks."

Dust swirled up around the ship as it settled to the ground with a rumble. After a moment, the air cleared. Billie had grown so accustomed to the drone of the engines that the silence seemed strange and empty.

"Tully?" said Ripley.

"Nada. If anyone's here, they're not moving."

"That door didn't explode by itself," said Brewster. "We should secure the area—"

"Me, take chances?" said Ripley. "Come on, folks, let's get armed."

Billie followed the others to the supply hold at the end of the corridor, heart pounding. One of those fliers was going to work. She was no pilot, but she had learned a lot watching Wilks; standard military fliers were designed to be operated by mainline field soldiers, not a particularly bright bunch on the average. They would be strictly automatic, coordinates and go. Billie had already borrowed the access code from the *Kurtz*'s computer and figured it should work; she would see what kind of timeline they had and take her chances.

Wilks passed out weapons to the crew while Ripley handed out extra clips and comsets.

"We start at the first building and work around," said Wilks, "marines up front—Moto, you're on point."

"Tully, I want you to stay onboard to monitor," said Ripley. "Jones, you watch the hatch. We're not going to be out of sight completely at any time, so just yell if you see anything Tully misses."

The doctor accepted his carbine tentatively.

"You know how to use it?" said Wilks.

"Yeah. Well, pretty much. I've never actually *fired* one, but we had a safety course in med school."

"Good enough," said Wilks.

"McQuade, Billie, you're covering our asses," said Ripley.

Billie and the captain nodded and slung their rifles.

"Once the area is secured, we'll come back for tools and then get to work on the detonator problem."

Tully walked back to control as the crew filed down to the APC dock. They stood at the hatch,

Moto, Wilks, and Brewster in front with their weapons ready.

Ripley put her hand on the door controls and looked at them. "Any questions?"

No one spoke. Billie took a deep breath as the deck fanned open.

26

Wilks stepped into the bright sunlight, crouched, his carbine pointed to one side of the ship.

Nothing. Moto would be trained on the structure in front of them, Brewster to the other side.

"How's it look?" he said into the 'com. He scanned the area for movement.

"Clear," said Tully.

"Go," said Wilks.

Moto jogged forward, weapon up, as Wilks and Brewster covered her. They were close enough to the dingy gray building that it only took half a minute. Moto leaned against the corner of the unit and crouched there.

"Go," said Wilks again. He and Brewster jogged across the dusty landing pad. Adrenaline sparked his senses; his heart thumped. He knew that Ripley and Falk had them covered, but that didn't make a run through open space in unswept territory any more comfortable. Then again, this was what he knew how to do best. It almost felt good.

They reached Moto and edged to the door of the building. Wilks held up his hand for the others to stay put behind them.

"I'll kick," he said. "Moto, you're high, Brewster low—on my mark."

The three of them stepped to the entry.

"Now!"

Wilks kicked. The door crashed inward. Brewster sidled into the entry in a crouch, Moto standing. They swept the room left to right and Wilks took in some air. It was a barracks and it looked deserted. A row of cots lined the far wall, interspaced with a series of tall cabinets that all stood open and empty. There were no other exits.

The room was in disarray, with blankets and articles of clothing scattered about, and the air smelled stale and musty. Dust motes swam in the beams of sunlight and resettled. Whatever had happened, they had missed it by weeks. Maybe months.

"Looks clean," said Wilks. Better, it *felt* clean.

Brewster straightened up and motioned toward the floor with his rifle. A series of bullet holes and chipped plastecrete ran in a line up the wall behind them. A smashed cot lay nearby. It looked like someone had tried unsuccessfully to barricade the door.

"Something went down, but it's old news," said Brewster quietly.

"Secured?" said Ripley through the 'com.

"Yeah." Wilks signed. "Only four more to go. And we should check the fliers and APC."

They backed out of the room.

Twenty minutes later, they were finished. There was a substantial amount of dried blood splashed in the mess hall, evidence of struggle in most of the structures, acid damage here and there, but no bodies and no apparent threat. Wilks felt the adrenaline seep from his system little by little, but he remained alert. Getting sloppy could cost.

As Ripley stood outside the ship and delegated responsibilities to the others, Wilks continued to scan the area. Not having a portable sensor was a bitch, although he found that as he got older, he didn't like to depend on mechanical augmentation as much. Earth had fallen to shit from too much greed and not enough humanity; the machines had just been fuel for the fire. As a young hotshot marine he had felt differently about things, but experience had taught him that nothing was infallible. . . .

Fucking middle age, he thought. *Maybe I should take up philosophy when this is over.*

If it was ever over. If they made it. The planet had become a dead end for billions of people; not so long ago, he had been a dead man walking on stolen time himself, but somewhere along the way that had changed. He was ready to play his part in the end, to finish it. . . .

"Ready," said Ripley. She started toward the hill.

"Ready," he replied, but not to anyone in particular. He started after her.

They stood at the base of the hill in front of the gate. The metal door looked as if it had been melted open with a welding device; it sported a huge gaping hole in the middle. Ripley had thought weapons fire when she had seen it from the *Kurtz*, but the edges of the hole were smooth. She wondered what exactly had gone on in the last hours here, before the scientists had been taken. . . .

Wilks stepped into the darkness first.

Ripley waited a few beats and then followed, pulled herself through the hole and took a breath. The air was thick with moisture and the smell of mold. Grayish-green moss and lichens had developed in scraggly patches along the inside of the gate. Nice place.

The small room she had stepped into led to a dark corridor; a mechanical door, stuck halfway open, separated the two.

"Talk to me, Wilks," she said.

"Got a straight walk ahead of you for ten meters, then a tee—the sign says 'armory' on the right and 'control' left. No sign of infestation, and the mold is pretty thick on either branch. I think we're alone."

Ripley let out her air and stepped around the broken door. "You heard him," she said. Moto and Tully came in behind her with the equipment cases.

"Let us know, Falk," she said softly. He would keep watch at the gate. Billie, McQuade, and the doctor were back at the *Kurtz*.

"Gotcha."

She directed her light forward as she moved down the dank hall. Wilks stood at the tee, weapon up, his face distorted in the swaying light.

"You stay here," he said. "I'll check control." His voice echoed with a faintly metallic ring.

Wilks moved off down the hall.

Ripley kept her weapon trained toward the armory, although Wilks was right—it didn't look like anyone had been here in months.

Anyone or any*thing*, she added mentally.

Moto and Tully waited with her. "Maybe the firing sequence was interrupted by some natural phenomenon," said Moto. She poked at a strand of damp moss on the wall. "These weapons were never meant to withstand exposure to the elements."

Wilks rejoined them. "Clear," he said. "Not a real complicated maze. Hall runs straight twenty meters and then elbows into control. Let me check the other side and we're set."

"I'll cover," said Ripley. "Tully, Moto, you go ahead."

Ripley clutched her weapon with damp palms—androids could sweat, after all—and waited for Wilks in the murky stillness. She was ready for this to be over with; she was tired of being looked to for answers. Billie was right—she *did* need to finish what she had started. But when it was done, she had a lot more shit to deal with. It seemed as though it would never end. . . .

Wilks moved back to join her.

"That didn't take long," she said.

"Same setup on this side, only the door is locked and sealed. Hasn't been opened in a while, either. I think the bombs are safe."

She smiled. "Great—safe bombs."

Wilks chuckled. "Yeah, funny. I—"

"Hey," Moto crackled into their ears, "looks like we got a little more than corrosion down here." She sounded worried. "I think someone tried to put a stop to this countdown permanently."

Billie sat in the control room of the *Kurtz* and listened to Ripley's report.

". . . we've localized the problem, but it's going to take longer than I'd hoped. Everything has been dislinked, and as far as we can tell, the main set of hardwiring was bollixed." Her voice was punctuated with heavy static; the 'coms weren't designed to send or receive through so many tons of rock.

"How long?" said Billie.

"We'll be lucky to get out of here by dark."

She continued to outline the situation, but Billie tuned it out. The sun was still high above; night was a good six hours away. Plenty of time.

She stood and stretched leisurely as Ripley cut off. "I'm going to take some food packets over," Billie said. "That should cheer them up."

McQuade grinned. "Or they might decide to blow us all to hell."

"Just don't give them any of the stir-fry and we're probably safe," said Jones. "Suicide *was* on my mind when I ate dinner."

Billie laughed.

"Want company?" said McQuade. "Jones could watch the sensors—"

"Nah." She hoped she sounded casual. "I'll only be a minute."

She walked back to the dining hall and gathered some of the self-heating packets and some utensils. She also stopped by the weapons stock for a few extra magazines before heading to the lower deck.

Taking a flier wouldn't jeopardize the mission; if she didn't make it back in time—well, she would just have to. She didn't expect them to wait for her.

Billie walked out of the APC dock and squinted in the bright light. The air was sweet and cool against her skin, a far cry from the canned recycled stuff that she was accustomed to. Insects and birds sang their songs in the trees around the compound. It was beautiful, what was left of it.

The firepower that the others were currently setting up would take out a big chunk of this entire region, as Ripley had explained it; but not right away.

"Six months?" Falk had said. "Why so fucking long?"

"It's a big planet. The aliens are all over it. Assuming they can swim—better, of course, if they can't and they drown—it'll take three or four months for them to *get* here. They could be 20,000 kilometers away, halfway around the planet. Allowing time for them to stop and eat and pee, six months should be plenty."

That had brought up a bunch of other questions: Why was the superqueen calling them? Maybe whoever made these war toys was coming to collect them, somebody—Wilks?—had said. Would they stay here once they arrived? Nobody knew. They had to go with what they had. They'd baited the trap and they had to allow time for the rats to get to the cheese. . . .

Billie shook the memory. Falk raised a hand as she approached.

"Brought you some lunch," she said.

"Oh, boy." He looked less than thrilled. "You gonna join us for the poisoning?"

"Nope. I thought I'd see if I could scavenge some supplies from a few of the buildings."

Falk took the assortment of foil pouches from her with a frown.

"I don't think that's such a good idea," he said. "Does Ripley know—?"

Billie shrugged. "Tell her if you want. I'm armed, the compound is empty, and McQuade is watching for activity." She tapped her headset. "Besides, I'm sick of sitting on my ass; thought I'd make myself useful."

"I hear that," said Falk. "Just be careful."

She smiled and walked away. The fliers were hidden from Falk's vantage point, two buildings away. She stepped out of view and picked up her pace a bit.

"What are you doing, Billie?" McQuade's voice spoke in her ear.

Falk spoke before she did. "Trying to find us some decent food instead of this swill," he said. "Surely you can't object to that?"

Thank you, Falk! She reached the first ship and looked inside; Wilks and the others had left the hatches popped open. The landhopper was tiny, made to accommodate a few people, with only minimal space and scant supplies. Her heart sank when she saw the ripped wires and broken plastic of the console.

"There's nothing in those ships but emergency rations," said McQuade. "Why don't you just get back here? I don't like the idea of you roaming around by yourself, and you could mess up my readings. The *Kurtz* isn't out of food—"

"I'm a big girl," said Billie as she moved to the second flier. She kept her movements casual; if McQuade saw her run, he'd sound an alarm. "I was actually looking for some more tools—"

"Billie, get back to the ship *now*," said Ripley. The edge in her voice was sharp, even through the static.

So much for playing it safe—

Billie stepped into the second flier and looked around. It seemed undamaged. She slid the hatch closed behind her and hurried to the pilot's seat. A few switches and the ship hummed to life.

"Dammit, Billie, talk to me! What the hell are

you doing? You can't *leave*; we don't have time for this!"

Billie ignored Ripley and fed the access codes and coordinates into the small computer. Thank Buddha for small favors, like nil security on the little ship. Plenty of fuel, automatic everything—

"Billie, wait!" It was Wilks. "I'll go with you, just hold on a minute—" At least he sounded more worried than angry.

"Sorry," she said. "This is the only way; I know she's not dead. I'll be back before dark if I can—"

Billie toggled the user-friendly controls and the flier began to lift. She understood most of the buttons and hoped that what she didn't know wouldn't hurt her. She yanked the headset off and threw it down as Ripley and the captain shouted at her and the small ship pivoted in the air.

She knew they were pissed, but they didn't need her to finish. Ripley's hatred was behind everything the older woman did; Billie was motivated by a feeling that seemed just as strong. Love?

She strapped in with a silent prayer as the flier rocketed south:

Please let this work.

27

"*Shit*," Ripley said. "I should have known, she *told* me she was going to do this."

Tully and Moto continued to strip wires in the dimly lit control room.

"Nothing we can do about it now," Wilks said. An icy hand had gripped his heart; he felt as frustrated as Ripley and sick with fear for the young woman. He had known Billie longer, had known how the 'casts of the lost family had eaten at her; if anyone was responsible, he was.

If you had been thinking, you could have stopped her.

Then it was Billie's voice he heard: *Fuck off, Wilks, who do you think you are?*

Wilks gritted his teeth. There *wasn't* anything

he could do. Just hope that Billie was going to come back. If anything happened to her, he'd—

What?

Nothing.

Ripley said, "You're right. I just wish . . ." She trailed off and absently picked up her spot welder.

"Hey, everyone there?" McQuade's voice crackled from the set. "I got movement here, coming from the west!"

Wilks unslung his rifle and started to the exit. "Falk?" he said as he ran.

"Nothing yet."

"Can't get a number," said McQuade. "They're moving in a group, five or six—"

Wilks reached the sliding door. Falk crouched in the small anteroom, shielded by the thick melted gate, weapon pointed out.

"They've stopped outside the compound," McQuade said. "Looks like—wait. Somebody's coming."

Wilks and Falk stood together and waited. "Everyone stay put," Wilks said.

A lone figure stumbled into view, halfway between the *Kurtz* and Orona's hill. A woman, unarmed. Her clothes were in rags, exposing one dirty breast. Her face was a mask of fear.

"Hello?" she called out, voice quaking. "Is anyone here?" She pushed stringy, matted hair out of her eyes and looked around nervously. "I'm safe! We've been waiting for a ship to come—" She

turned and held outstretched arms toward the
Kurtz, palms up. "Please!"

"Wilks?" Falk whispered. He lowered his rifle
slightly.

"I dunno." He looked at the woman. Yelled:
"Bring the others out into the open!"

She spun at the sound of his voice, but kept her
arms up. Her face twisted and she began to sob.
"Yes," she said, "of course!"

Two men and another woman walked into view,
as tattered and grubby as the first person. They
all looked frightened and unsure of themselves.
None of them were armed.

"McQuade? Is that it?" Wilks asked.

A pause. "Can't tell. Nothing else moving."

The four stood in the open. They swayed
slightly, as if holding themselves up was an effort.

"You catching this, Ripley?" said Wilks.

"Yeah." She sounded worried. "I don't like it;
could be trouble."

"We got 'em covered," said Falk. "What say I
step outside and see? If they got friends in the
bushes, they won't fire on their own people—"

Wilks tightened his jaw. "They might."

"We could stay in here and talk about it all
day," Falk said, "but eventually we're going to
have to go back to the ship. Gotta do something
with 'em."

Wilks nodded. He didn't like it either, but Falk
was right. "Stay low and give me a clear sight," he
said.

Falk raised his voice. "Okay, I'm coming out
now! We have loaded weapons, so don't move!"

The first woman continued to sob, the only noise in the still air. Falk climbed through the gate, carbine trained on the ragged group. He moved toward them slowly and carefully.

Wilks put one leg through the gate and straddled it. He pointed his rifle at the clump of trees on the west—

The four people suddenly hit the ground as one, the quiet shattered as gunfire cracked across the compound.

Billie looked at the computer readings as the flier sped toward the state that had been Northern California, but she didn't touch anything. It all seemed fine; she would be at the coordinates in a little under two hours, provided nothing went wrong. . . .

What could go wrong? I'm a top-notch pilot and Amy and her family will be standing by, waiting to jump onboard when I show up. Plus I have lots of time.

She smiled at herself. She had apparently gone insane at some point and hadn't noticed until now. When she had committed herself to saving the child back on Gateway, she'd never thought she'd be doing it this way—alone in a stolen ship. She couldn't remember *what* she had thought—

That it would be easy, maybe. That someone else would do it for me.

If she had learned anything from knowing Ripley, it was that to make something happen, *you* had to make it happen; silly and redundant, but very true. She couldn't just sit and hope that things would change by themselves.

Not anymore. The little girl's name was Amy, but it was also Billie; they would make it together or not at all.

Shit—

Wilks hit the ground. He didn't see the shooters, but he capped off a short burst into the trees at chest level. The hillside provided partial protection; he didn't dare move—

McQuade shouted in his ear, most of it lost in the noise. "...fuckin' two gunners, due—"

The metal gate clanged as bullets drilled into it.

Wilks fired again and spared a glance at Falk. He was down—hit, or had he purposely dropped? No way to know—

The four fanatics remained still, but one of the men began to shout. "Don't kill them, we need them, She demands them—"

The other three began to screech for salvation, calling loudly on the Great Mother.

Oh, man! They were pinned down; they had to do something to break this up.

Another barrage of fire *chinged* into the gate. Wilks got an idea. He screamed and lay still, pretending to be wounded.

Don't move, Falk, if you're alive, don't move!

Seconds ticked by. Wilks stared into the bushes and waited. Sweat trickled down his neck as the sun suddenly seemed to get much hotter. He heard quiet movement behind him, from inside the gate, and hoped that Ripley had the sense to stay put.

The four fanatics continued to pray in high, shaky voices.

Wilks heard twigs crackle and snap ahead of him. A dark shape moved through the woods.

"Not *yet!*" a voice tried to hiss from several meters farther into the trees. "Wait!"

Two gunners. Wilks aimed at the shape in front and fired a double tap.

The figure fell back into the shadows with a yelp.

Wilks retrained his rifle at the voice and squeezed the trigger again. The unseen sniper cried out in pain.

At the sound of the shots, the people lying next to Falk jumped up and ran toward Wilks. One of them tripped over Falk's body and smacked into the dirt.

Falk rolled over, sat up, and cracked the man's skull with the butt of his rifle.

Way to go, Falk!

Wilks fired twice more. Both of the women crumpled.

The last man stumbled onward, eyes crazed. He got close enough so that gore spattered Wilks as his final shot caught the runner in the chest. The man fell, coughed blood, and died.

"Hold it!" Wilks shouted.

Nothing moved. If the gunners were still alive, there was no sign. He came up slowly, rifle still aimed into the trees.

"Falk, you hit?" he said into the 'com.

The big man had lain back down. "Yeah. Not too bad, I don't think." His voice shook.

"Ripley?"

"Right here. Did you get them?" She didn't sound too steady either.

"Pretty sure." He wiped at the bits of tissue and blood on his skin. "That, or I shot a couple of innocent bystanders; let me check. Hang in there, Falk."

"I'm not going anywhere."

Wilks pulled into a crouch and ran low for the trees, weapon ready. If anybody moved, he or she was going to get pasted.

One of the shooters was dead, a middle-aged man with a shaved head. He'd been shot in the throat. The other was still alive, a few meters away, a small woman with a bad stomach wound. The bullets had ripped her gut to shreds. Amazingly, she was still conscious; she lay on her back and pushed at the dirt with her bare feet, trying to crawl away from the compound. She opened her eyes as Wilks approached, her face contorted with pain and rage, her abdomen a slick red tangle of exposed intestine.

"You'll—die—" she managed. "You'll—" She closed her eyes, exhausted.

It was cool in the shade of the trees; a light breeze stalled the sweat on Wilks's brow as he aimed carefully. "Yeah," he said.

The shot echoed for a long time.

Tully worked at her portable console while Ripley continued to hook the system back together in the dim light. The original detonator was set up on a sequential timer, too complicated to fix easily, so Tully worked on a chain-link relay. The hardwiring had to be clean; it had to last for a while.

Falk was okay. He had two wounds, a minor one high in the left shoulder and a slightly more serious one through the meat of his bicep. Jones had already patched him up and filled him with painkillers.

Ripley worked as quickly as she could, aware that this first trouble wouldn't be their last if they didn't hurry.

"Ready," Tully said. "We still have to tune Orona's dish to where we're gonna be when we reach a safe distance, but the program is set. In theory, we call the computer here and the clock starts running when we send the signal."

Ripley looked at the small console and nodded.

"Go try it," she said. "We don't want to count on theory."

"Right. I'll type in a command and send it. If the word shows on the screen, we have a clean signal."

"Go."

Tully grabbed a light and disappeared into the dark corridor.

Ripley stared at the jumble of wires and sighed. She didn't want to think about it, no time, but—

She had fired on the people who had run toward the gate. Meaning she wasn't First Lawed, a mandatory feature in synthetics. It was almost enough to make her believe that somehow it wasn't true, that Jones had misread the tests. Except she had never taken any kind of electronics course in her life and she knew exactly what went where; the knowledge was just *there*, like how to walk or speak. She wondered what else she knew. . . .

"Ripley?" It was Tully, her voice barely audible.

"Do it," she said into the set. She turned toward the portable and watched. A series of numbers ran across the screen and disappeared. A second passed, and the word "boom" appeared in the upper left corner in glowing green letters.

Ripley nodded. "It works."

Static intertwined with Tully's laughter, making Ripley suddenly feel very far away from everything. From humanity.

She got back to work.

Only a few minutes until landing. Billie watched the computer screen nervously and checked the action on her carbine for the hundredth time.

The ship began a gradual descent through the outskirts of an industrial town. She had flown over several small cities, had watched for signs of life all along the way; she'd seen plenty. Hundreds, thousands of aliens had run beneath her, headed north; there had been no people.

Billie hoped that the others were doing well. She also hoped that she wasn't about to crash. She rested her hands on the steering and pulled left a hair; the ship pulled left. She pushed forward and the ship nosed downward a bit.

Okay, got it—

The monitor blinked that the desired coordinates had been reached. If Amy's father had given out the wrong numbers in that last transmission, she was screwed. The flier's landing engines kicked on and it began to lower straight down. Billie maneuvered the ship over a strip of road. Rubble flew in the wake of the ship as it settled onto the pavement.

Billie unbuckled her safety straps and switched the engines off, amazed that it had been so easy. There was no movement outside the flier.

She patted the extra magazines and set of flaresticks in her hip pouch as she walked to the hatch and tried to ignore the fear. That the flying had been so simple somehow made it worse, like she had used up her luck.

Amy is the thing, she told herself firmly, *Amy and her father and Mordecai, and whoever else has become the girl's family.*

She stepped out of the flier, weapon raised, and immediately recoiled from the smell. The stench of burnt plastic and rot was overwhelming; maybe it was like that in all of the cities now. But the debris wasn't too bad, at least. Apparently there were still a few places that hadn't been destroyed completely by riots or infestation.

She walked around the ship. There was no sound, no motion; it was as if she were the only living being in an empty world. The buildings around her were all a uniform beige, and silent.

Where to start? She walked toward the structure to her right and read the lettering set above the smashed door frame. ENDOTECH MICRO. That sure sounded like a microchip company, and that's what the transmission had said, right? This had to be the place.

Unfortunately, the same lettering was on the building across the street. It was an entire complex, not one factory. Damn.

The silence was unnerving. Billie stepped through the door frame. Her boots crunched on bits of shattered plexi material as she looked up and down the entryway; halls led off into blackness in either direction.

Maybe she could find a control room of some kind with a working intercom system, or a speaker she could hook up to the flier. . . .

Brilliant. Except what the fuck do you know about wiring something like that up?

If she could fly a ship, she could figure it out. She sure as hell didn't have time to search each building—

Billie pulled a flarestick from her pocket and snapped it. The tip sizzled red—a dim light at best, but it'd have to do; if there had been a portable light onboard the flier, she hadn't seen it. She kicked herself for not thinking of it back at the compound as she stared into the pitch hallway, but there was nothing to be done about it now.

She started down the corridor to her left. Her

footsteps echoed loudly and hollowly in the cool, dead air—if anyone was in the building, she wasn't going to be a surprise to them.

Within seconds, the light from the outside had disappeared completely. The glow from the flare only illuminated the space a meter or two ahead. She walked close to one wall, held the light up to make out the words on the doors she passed— mostly names of employees, it seemed.

The hallway seemed to go on forever. She struggled to damp down a feeling of dread that threatened to rise up and bloom into panic. The stale air was clammy against her skin; she didn't know where she was headed; anything could be waiting for her, watching her—and it was dark. That was the worst; it was blacker than space—

She stopped. This was completely stupid. She would go back outside and reevaluate the situation, she was going to lose it in here—

Suddenly she heard a noise directly behind her. *Snick.*

She froze. Just a little sound, *could be anything, a shift of weight or—*

The sound of a door opening.

Billie threw the flarestick to the ground and stepped on it. It dimmed, but didn't go out entirely. The flickering glow made the shadows dance wildly. She gritted her teeth against a scream, her eyes wide and useless in the dark. She turned slowly, as quietly as she could, her brain yammering a thousand things at once.

Human, not a drone, fanatic maybe, do I talk or wait? Are they armed? Oh, shit, oh Amy—

She pointed the carbine ahead of her and tried to think clearly—

—until a pair of rough hands brushed against her face—

28

The sound came up so gradually it took Wilks a while to realize he was hearing it and what it was.

He had taken over Falk's position outside the armory and watched as the shadows lengthened across the compound. Moto went back to work with the others after Jones assured them Falk was okay. Wilks couldn't seem to focus on much of anything except Billie; McQuade was still monitoring the sensor readings and Ripley had as much help as she needed, so Wilks leaned against the gate and waited for Billie to get back.

And wondered if she ever would.

McQuade picked up a ship to the east, too big

to be the landhopper that Billie had taken. It had set down not far from where they had dropped the mother queen. Apparently there were pilots in the fanatic crowd, and none too smart. The bugs weren't going to be separating the followers from the baby food for long once they started arriving in big numbers.

Now he focused on the sound. Kind of a high, keening wail, a faint whine.

"Hurry, Ripley," he said into the 'com. "They're coming."

Billie screamed and jerked the trigger. The blackness broke and re-formed around the bursts of gunfire, the sound deafening in the corridor as the bullets hit the wall. She fell to the floor and scrabbled backward on her elbows after catching a glimpse of tattered clothing—

"Oh, God, don't shoot! Stop!" A man's voice. "Please, I'm sane, I'm sane!"

He sounded as terrified as she felt. Billie held still so that he wouldn't have a target and trained her carbine at the voice. She held her fire as the man babbled on.

"Please, I have to find her, don't kill me—"

Her. The word sank in and footsteps suddenly crashed through the hallway as he ran away from Billie, back toward the entry.

"Wait!" she shouted. "Amy!"

The footsteps stopped. He spoke again, pathetically eager. "You've seen her? Please, where is she? Who are you?"

Billie stood up. "Walk toward the exit," she said. "I've got my gun on you, so don't make any sudden moves."

As she followed his footsteps down the corridor, the full impact of his words sank in. He knew Amy.

An old, white-haired man with a ragged beard stepped into the light filtering in through the broken door. Deep lines of fear and worry creased his brow. Billie moved up to meet him.

"It's you," she said, "—your transmissions— where is Amy?"

His eyes widened. "You saw them? We had hoped that someone—" He broke off. Then: "They took her, two days ago. Mordecai was killed trying to stop them, the lunatics—she's gone. I don't even know if she's alive—" Tears welled in his eyes.

Billie felt sick. Two days! "Where did they take her?"

"There are underground tunnels throughout the complex," he said. "They have Amy with the others, part of their food or breeding stock, there's a nest at the east end—" He spoke quickly, tried to say everything at once. "I've been trying to get in but I *can't*, there were drone guards and today they started running away, north, and I heard ships, I heard your ship—"

"Take me there," said Billie. If Amy was still alive, maybe she'd be in the nest, waiting to be implanted . . . maybe most of the guards would be on their way to the queen. True, there'd probably be a few left behind to guard the eggs that were still unhatched, but maybe it wasn't over yet.

Ripley had fucked up.

They pulled the control board from the wall and she worked over the dismantled pieces and stripped wires for hours. It had to go sequentially, A to B to C and so on, or the hidden bombs, some of them kilometers away, wouldn't all detonate; rewire the wrong way and the first explosion could knock the system apart. That wouldn't do at all.

It had been going fine. Tully and Moto had both finished their jobs and she was almost finished—when she suddenly discovered that something was missing. She was halfway through the seventh switch before she realized that she had run out of board to work on and she needed more.

"No," she said. She checked and rechecked; the third panel had been misdirected to the fifth. She would have to pull it loose and rewire it. It would take another two hours.

How long before the first group of drones reached the compound? Maybe long after dark. Or maybe five minutes from now . . .

She pulled the switch loose and started over. If she had to stay on Earth to finish it, she would. It didn't matter if she died—as long as the alien bitch and her children were destroyed along with her.

● ● ●

Billie and the old man crept down the stairwell together, the walls lined thickly with alien secretions. The main nest was in the basement of a structure only two blocks from the ship.

They had run in the dwindling light together through the empty streets, had stopped for him to tie a rag-torch before stepping into the silent building.

He held the torch high as they edged down the steps. The flame reflected off the dark, shiny substance and created a flickering illusion that the stairs themselves were alive. With each footfall the structure moved and shifted; it seemed as if they were stepping on alien bodies about to rise up—

It got hotter as they moved toward the nest; they rounded the landing and started the next flight down. A half-open door webbed with cobby spittle stood at the bottom.

A low moan, human, drifted up to greet them, followed by a chittering sigh. They stopped a few steps from the bottom. Sweat ran down Billie's spine.

"I never got this far," whispered the old man.

Billie kept her carbine trained on the door and willed her legs to move forward. The nest wouldn't be completely deserted, of course—someone had to watch the eggs—but Ripley had figured that into the time delay—

The door flung open and a drone leaped for them—

Billie fired. The thing screamed, its teeth

gnashing as its chest shattered. Acid hissed and bubbled, ate into the plastecrete.

A second howling creature catapulted over the first.

Billie's shots ripped open the long skull; its jaw dropped open and kept dropping as it fell onto the stairs. More alien blood spattered.

The old man cried out and there was a third—

It loomed in the doorway and hissed, kicked at the fallen sibling in front of it to get to them—

Billie depressed the trigger. One of the bullets hit at an angle and sparked, a tiny fire in the gloom.

The creature fell back and Billie stumbled over the dead drone at her feet to get to the door, the old man behind her.

"Don't step in the blood!" she said.

Billie lunged into the basement and fired; alien cries blended with the explosions of the carbine. The noise pounded her ears.

Dark figures darted toward her as she shot again and again—

Her left calf was on fire, the pain deep and intense—

The old man's light flickered on behind her, just in time for her to see a grinning drone clap a talon on her shoulder. Its inner set of teeth shot out of the gaping mouth and she screamed, jammed her carbine into its gut. The shots blew its abdomen out behind it. The thing's claw ripped at her flesh, tore her coverall and some of her skin, but released her and fell away. . . .

Billie panted, whipped her carbine left to right.

Nothing else came at her, nothing moved. Her skin was blistered from the blast of close gunfire; her ears rang. Acid had touched her leg and she felt her blood run from the chemical burn, but she was still standing.

The guards were all dead.

They were in a small room. The torch chased shadows in the slimy den, a dozen or so eggs in the center, most peeled open. Dim figures were strung to the walls in various stages of decay; a few looked alive, unconscious. Spidery dead larvae littered the floor and the place reeked of rotten flesh.

"Amy—" said the old man. He stepped past Billie. She felt a scream rise up when she saw what he moved toward.

A small figure roped to the wall, head down, short reddish hair—

What had been a person moaned, lifted its face to the light. . . .

An emaciated young man, his skin cracked, one eye swollen closed. Drool ran down his bearded chin.

He grinned at the old man, his puffy tongue hanging out. "I'm pregnant," he croaked, words slurred. Caked blood nestled in the corners of his mouth.

"Where are they?" said Billie, her voice shrill. "Where's Amy?"

The man's head lolled forward. Amy's father

grabbed his hair and jerked his head back, held the torch close to the dying man's face.

"Presents," he said. A bubble of pus in one nostril popped open; the liquid ran over his scabbed lips. "The Chosen—breeders flew away—serve the Mother"—the word came out *muder*—"flew to oneness . . . revelation. She waits—"

"No," Billie said. The ships that the old man had heard—

He turned to her, awful realization on his tired face.

". . . the holy land . . ." rasped the fanatic.

"She's lost," said the old man. His voice hitched.

"Stand back," said Billie. She rammed a new magazine into her rifle and tossed the empty to the floor. "I know where they went."

And they would go there: Orona's mountain, the holy land—

But first things first.

Billie pointed the carbine and pulled the trigger.

The howls of the closing army were nearer, more distinct now. He knew it took thousands of the bugs to make that kind of noise; Wilks scanned the skies as the minutes stretched by, the compound bathed in reddish twilight. If Billie didn't return soon—

The *Kurtz* could circle and wait for a while, but they only had so much fuel. And they couldn't stay put with that many aliens on their way.

Thinking about it, Wilks realized they had made a mistake. They should have wired the bombs first, parked the ship with the queen somewhere else to draw the brood, then dropped her off after things were ready. They hadn't thought it out right, hadn't expected the damned things to come so fast, for there to be so many of them from that direction—

Shit, shit, shit—

"Done!" Ripley said.

Wilks took a deep breath and let it out slowly. He knew Ripley would wait until the last possible second to pull out, but that second seemed much closer suddenly—and it was almost dark.

"Wilks! Company, due west, *now*!" McQuade shouted.

Wilks pointed his rifle at the trees and yelled through the gate. "Ripley, Moto, let's move!"

An unseen alien screamed from nearby as Moto and then Ripley stumbled through the hole in the door. They dropped the tool cases and unslung their carbines.

As a unit, the three of them moved toward the ship.

The woods crashed and crunched with the sounds of movement, but there was still nothing to see—

The first drone broke from the trees and ran into the compound, its long body hunched, arms extended. It was going to see the queen, but they were between it and her.

All three of them fired at once. The thing

shrieked and hit the ground, nearly cut in two by the armor-piercing bullets.

The forest suddenly erupted, spewed forth a handful of the drones at once. They loped for the threesome, howled as the rain of bullets found them.

"Come *on*!" someone shouted behind them.

It was Falk. He stood in the hatchway of the *Kurtz*, bandaged arm limp, rifle extended with his good arm.

"*Go*," Ripley said. She stood her ground, continued to fire as more of the drones ran into view.

Wilks and Moto ran the few meters to the ship as Ripley and Falk covered.

Wilks spun in the open hatch and fired. Dozens more of the bugs came out of the trees, their insane bodies moving at great speed—

"Ripley!" he yelled.

She backed to the *Kurtz* without looking and nearly tripped on the deck. Wilks took out three more of the creatures as she turned and stumbled inside.

Falk hit the button. The hatch slid up and in, too slow. Wilks crouched down and fired as several of the bugs scrabbled to get in. One of the drones grabbed at the barrel of his rifle just before the deck shut. He shot its glistening teeth through the back of its skull.

Tiny molten flecks peppered Wilks's cheeks.

But they were all inside. A score of aliens pounded at the closed hatch, their cries muffled through the alloy.

"McQuade, Brewster, get us out of here!"
Ripley yelled into her set.

Wilks slammed a fist against the hatch.

Billie was too late.

29

The flier descended slowly over the trees.

Despair washed over Billie at the sight of the empty compound—well, almost empty. Even in the heavy dusk she could see the dark, alien bodies strewn on the ground.

"Oh, no," she said softly.

The old man clenched his hands and said nothing. She had explained the situation on the way. Since the coordinates were preset and neither of them was a pilot, they'd had to return to the compound first; Billie had hoped that the *Kurtz*'s computer could help them locate Amy's ship, but now—

They'd had to leave, there'd been no choice, she told herself over and over.

In spite of what she knew to be the truth, a knot formed in her throat; she had been abandoned. Ripley had finished the detonator and the *Kurtz* had left. They would die.

Billie swallowed hard as the ship settled gently to the ground. She had made her decision and had no alternative but to accept the results.

"I'm sorry," she said. She didn't look at him, didn't want to see the pain on his face as their mutual hope died.

"It's not your fault," he said, his voice dull. "You tried. I—I'm glad it'll be over soon."

"We could try to escape the blast," she said, but disregarded the words as she spoke them. Where would they go? The planet would be dead, was already dead—

"Amy was all I had," he said. "It doesn't matter."

Tears finally spilled down Billie's cheeks and she nodded. She understood.

She turned to him, not certain of what to say—

And heard the sound of engines overhead.

Her heart pounded as she grabbed for the comset by her feet and held the plug to her ear.

". . . in, Billie! Talk to me!" It was Brewster.

Her tears turned to relieved sobs as the old man put his arm around her and laughed out loud.

"No," said Ripley. "We have to get out of here, now. If the things come back and start poking around the compound, they could mess up the bombs. I'm sorry."

Jesus, what a shitty deal, she thought. She *was* sorry; but the truth was that someone had to keep the priorities straight.

The *Kurtz*'s engines were cycling. Ripley stood in the APC bay with Billie and the old man, had listened to their story with mixed emotions. The initial happiness that Billie had returned had been replaced by frustration and disbelief. And a horrible, dreadful sense of nostalgia.

"You don't have to wait for us," said Billie. She wiped at her tear-stained face roughly, like a child, but stood tall. "Just help us find the ship. You can do that with the computer in a minute."

"And then what?" said Ripley. "You're going to set down in the middle of 10,000 drones on the chance that she's alive? I understand *why*, I know how it feels, but that's suicide!"

Ripley knew that she was right, but suddenly didn't want to meet Billie's gaze. *Did* she remember how it felt?

Fucking hypocrite. What had happened to her? All she wanted now was to destroy the breed that had destroyed her life—by taking her daughter.

"Maybe you can leave without her," Billie said. "I can't."

Ripley didn't speak, her thoughts jumbled. Her goal was to kill the creatures. Once upon a time, there had been other goals. Back when she still cared . . .

She looked up at Billie and saw a very familiar face.

"A ship set down about ten klicks east a few

hours ago," she said. Her mind began to clear as she spoke.

Ripley turned to the old man. "Can you handle a military carbine?"

"My eyesight isn't so good," he said, "but I can probably hold my own."

Ripley shook her head. "This isn't going to be a few drones, and it won't be easy in the dark." She paused. "I guess I'll have to go with you," she said to Billie.

Wilks watched as Ripley gathered extra magazines and two portable lamps from supply and felt the anger build. Finally, he couldn't stand it.

"You're out of your fucking minds!" He searched for words, frustrated. "Think about it!"

Ripley spoke over her shoulder as if she hadn't heard him. "Stay here as long as you can, then put down somewhere safe nearby. We'll come back here. If we haven't shown on the sensors in an hour, you get to be in charge again."

She turned, faced him, expression set. "Don't fuck it up."

He wanted to scream. When McQuade had spotted Billie's flier, something inside of him had—*released*; that was the only word he could put to it. And now Billie *and* Ripley were about to go try and kill themselves.

No. Stop this.

"I'll come with you," he said. "At least let me do that—"

"No," said Ripley calmly. She shouldered her rifle. "Someone's got to make sure things get finished."

"You can start the timer going now," he said. "In six months it goes off, we don't have to wait—"

"Wilks—" Ripley began.

"She's not your kid!" he tried.

Billie and Ripley looked at each other and then at Wilks. "Yeah, she is," Billie said. "She's ours."

Ripley said, "Besides, we don't have any room."

"That's bullshit! There's—"

"Cut it, Wilks. We're going, you're not."

He followed them down the steps and into the APC bay and tried to think of something else to say. The old man waited there. Moto stood nearby with a rifle.

"Ready?" said Billie.

The old man touched her arm. "I wish I could be of more help," he said. He started to say something else, then fell silent.

Billie nodded. Ripley handed her a lamp as Moto stepped to the entry button.

Wilks looked at Billie. He wasn't sure how he felt, didn't know what could happen between them in the right circumstances, but—

She looked back at him, obviously prepared for some kind of plea. Defiant, strong—

"Please come back," he said to her. "You have to come back, kid, because . . . because—"

She put her fingers on his lips. "I know, David."

Christ, he felt as if he were going to cry. He turned to Ripley. "Be careful," he said.

She nodded at him.

The door opened and they were gone.

They flew to the east without speaking. Billie was scared but determined, and she could see that Ripley felt the same way. There was nothing to say.

The flier's lights illuminated very little of the landscape, a blanket of trees and the peaks of the hills.

As they got closer to the queen's mountain, the noise increased, making the situation pretty damned clear. The combined hisses and howls of the monsters almost drowned out the ship's engines as they circled the peak.

Billie drew in a ragged breath as the flier's lights lit the ground. The circle of light was filled with moving black shapes.

"The ship is a little farther east," said Ripley. "Maybe it won't be so bad."

"Maybe," said Billie. She had never been much on gods, given her upbringing, but she prayed to any that might exist that Amy was still alive.

Ripley vaguely remembered some part of a quote as she maneuvered the ship toward the small peak in front of them. How did it go? Into the valley of death rode the six hundred...?

Below, maybe 100,000 of the queen's children screeched, a roiling sea of deadly, mindless monsters. She wondered what was on the agenda for their convention, if they had any idea what they were doing here or what was going to happen to them. And she wondered how many more there were to come.

They skimmed the peak and Ripley slowed the flier. They didn't have to search, at least. The land was flat here, some kind of recreational area gone to seed. The ship was in plain view, directly starboard.

Dozens of the drones ran west through the light of the descending ship. Ripley edged the hopper as close as she could to the larger ship and set it down.

The pounding started almost immediately. Through the shield dark figures continued to stream past, their cries Dopplering away.

Both of them stood and moved toward the hatch.

"We stick together," said Ripley. "Get inside, find her, back out."

Billie nodded, her cheeks flushed.

She's probably dead, thought Ripley, but didn't say it. After all, so where they.

She slid the hatch aside.

The doors of the ships faced one another, both open.

Billie leapt from the flier and faced east. She depressed the trigger without aiming; it wasn't necessary. A wall of creatures ran into the blasts and fell, sprayed acid and bits of exoskeleton behind them.

Ripley jumped with her and fired repeatedly into the oncoming tide of drones.

An alien skittered across the top of the flier and

prepared to lunge. Billie smashed in its chest with a short burst.

They sidestepped to the breeder ship, weapons on full auto. Enough of the things had dropped to create an obstacle; more monsters clambered over their fallen siblings to be slaughtered.

Billie ejected a spent magazine and slammed in another, just in time to pick another creature off the roof of the ship. The explosive bullets were shattering the things, and still they screamed and charged.

When they hit the entry of the breeder ship, Ripley covered as Billie moved inside.

A drone shrieked, reached for Billie from inside the doorway—

She sprayed it with steel and its acidic blood spewed and bubbled the wall—

The alien cries quieted abruptly as Ripley slammed the hatch closed.

Billie moved into the hold. Dim emergency lighting, two exits, there didn't seem—

A creature howled and emerged from one of the hallways in a crouch, cramped by the two-meter-high ceiling—

Ripley blasted it.

The monster's head blew apart; its arms flailed for another second before it realized it was dead and fell to the floor.

They scanned the room for more. Billie took in the human blood that painted the interior, the articles of shredded clothing that lay about. And the bodies.

"Amy!" she screamed.

It had been a massacre. Billie counted twenty humans, maybe more, in a tangled heap in a corner of the room. Some had been ripped apart—there she saw a naked arm separated from its torso, here a disembodied leg. . . .

She stepped over the serrated tail of one of the dead bugs and screamed again. "Amy!"

No response. There was only the pounding of her heart, matched by the pounding cries of the alien sea behind them.

Ripley took in the destruction, the wasted life that littered the ship, her mind in overdrive. She had been here before. . . .

Billie took a step toward what was probably the control area and called for the girl again. Nothing. The young woman approached the heap of corpses, searched for the lost child in their midst. Ripley kept her rifle trained on the door closest to Billie.

It's better if she's dead than taken—But her heart wrenched as Billie let out a cry and fell to her knees before the pile, her face gray.

"No, no, no—" Billie repeated the word again and again as she reached through the tangle of limbs—

—and the hatch behind them pulled loose with a metallic screech and monstrous cries filled the room—

Billie was nauseated. The people must have huddled together at the end as they attempted to fend off an attack. At least two of the dead still clutched weapons—had the breeders gotten control? Or had the fanatics finally understood that the creatures didn't give a shit about *any* human life?

It didn't matter, none of it. She felt a blind second of hope as she looked quickly at each body.

A small face, flecked with gore, eyes closed, half beneath the body of a tattered corpse. Billie felt her legs buckle; words of denial came from far away, from her.

Amy.

Billie shoved at the bodies, placed a shaky hand on the tiny brow. Oh, God, Amy—

The little girl's eyes flickered open.

Gunfire roared.

Ripley spun and fired. Two meters away, a drone's grin melted and ran. A speckle of burning acid hit Ripley's arm as she shot again; another bug's chest exploded into black shards. She backed up a step as a third creature ducked toward her from the stream outside—

"Billie!" she yelled. She opened fire; the blasts took the bug at its thighs, the limbs skittered away from its torso, and still it reached—

The thing's arms flew back as Billie stepped beside her and shot its abdomen to bits. A scream—

Amy?

The scream was human, a child's. A red-haired girl clung to Billie and cried out, the sound lost as the weapons thundered.

Ripley moved forward again. They had to get

back to the flier, back past the relentless wash of death—

—her rifle clicked empty as a taloned claw shot through the entry and grabbed at her—

—and Billie fired, sent alien shrapnel flying as Ripley jammed a new magazine into her carbine—

It had to be now.

"I'll cover!" Ripley shouted. "Go!"

She jumped out into the darkness. She sprayed bullets, cut at the things. She was dimly aware that Billie and the girl were ducking behind her toward the flier, was dimly aware that she was screaming—a hoarse cry of rage from deep inside. All thought was gone, blotted out by the hatred that controlled her, that pulled the trigger—

They ran toward the flier, almost there—

Billie slapped at the external control. The hatch opened.

The girl stumbled, fell into the flier. Billie was right behind her, Ripley almost on top of them. Ripley spun, hosed her weapon back and forth, sleeting death on full auto—

The hatch closed as her weapon ran dry.

The ship rocked from side to side as the aliens swarmed over and around it, howled and hit.

The girl huddled against the wall and sobbed.

Billie crooned at the girl: "It's okay, Amy, it's okay, it's okay—"

Ripley ran to the pilot's seat and fumbled with the controls. There was a splintering crash from behind, then another.

They're tearing the goddamn walls—

"Hang on!" Ripley screamed.

The engine whined and groaned. And lifted the ship several meters before letting it crash back to the ground.

The impact dropped Billie to the floor. She turned to the child, who trembled and cried but didn't seem injured.

Too much weight—

The flier couldn't lift with the monsters still clinging to it, screaming—

There was a wrenching crack from the rear. A jagged, gaping hole appeared in the wall. Black taloned arms pulled at the edges, widened it. A strange, oily smell filled the small ship.

Billie aimed at the hole as a great black skull, teeth dripping, hissed and craned into the flier.

"Billie, no! Don't—"

Billie fired. The drone vanished—and the entire rear of the little ship exploded into flames.

Ripley smelled the fuel and turned; the fuckers must have ruptured the tank—

She saw Billie point her weapon.

"Billie, no! Don't shoot!"

The words were lost as a great flash of heat washed over Ripley. Billie was thrown backward; the little girl tumbled with her to the front.

Aliens shrieked outside.

Fuck—!

Ripley ran to the hatch, weapon extended, and hit the control. Nothing. Electrical and hydraulics were shot, the door jammed.

The fire spread toward them, licked up the walls as the air became thick with greasy smoke. They were going to fry, unless—

She triggered the explosive bolts and the hatch fell away. Cool air rushed in.

Billie staggered over, coughing, one arm around the child.

They had to make it back to the breeder ship and pray that it would make air—

Ripley raised her weapon and stepped back into the middle of the nightmare.

Billie hustled Amy out the door in front of her. She searched the darkness wildly for targets, but the creatures were preoccupied with the flames. A drone fell toward them with a scream, its spindly torso coated and consumed with fire. Bright orange crackled up its dark body as it writhed on the ground. Other aliens drenched in flaming fuel ran from the ship, living torches.

Amy screamed and pointed to the roof of the breeder ship. Billie aimed as a monster flung itself toward them, shot it. The creature clattered to the ground.

"Move!" shouted Ripley. She ran for the breeder ship, firing occasional bursts of ammo at the creatures that still ran at them.

There were at least a dozen caught in the explosion. The huge bugs danced and hissed, lit the night with their fire-soaked movements. The air had heated to blistering—and the creatures had ceased attacking.

They didn't like fire, Billie remembered.

She and Amy followed Ripley back onto the breeder ship.

Stupid, stupid—! Ripley had tried to warn her; she should have known the smell of fuel.

"Watch the door!" Ripley yelled. She ran for the control room. Billie aimed at the broken hatch, her vision blurred from the heat and sweat.

Amy screamed behind her—

Billie pivoted, saw the drone rise up from behind the form-chairs and reach for Amy—

The spray of bullets batted it down. Amy cried out again, looked past Billie—

—and Billie spun just in time to see a scrabbling shape, coated with fire and screeching, run into the entry and jump for her.

There was a dead man in the pilot's chair, his throat torn out.

Ripley kicked at him. The body slid to the floor with a thump. She dropped into the seat, stabbed at the controls, and the ship's engines coughed to life.

Relief, cool and welcome, flooded over her.

She heard the little girl scream, heard Billie's weapon rumble and roar as she continued to check the readings. Hardly enough fuel to take off, recyclers down, landing gear disabled, shields missing—they'd be lucky to move at all.

Just a little, just enough, just get us out of here—

Amazed, Ripley discovered she didn't want to die.

•   •   •

The creature fell toward Billie; its dying claws clutched at her torn coverall. Hot pain as the fire burned her arms and chest—

She rammed the weapon out, jerked the trigger—

The monster flew back, sprayed pieces of burning shell. Billie slapped at the fire on her clothes, the stench of burned flesh and hair her own. She dry-heaved once with pain and the odors of cooked skin—

The ship jerked suddenly beneath her feet. Billie stumbled backward and fell.

"Hold tight!" she shouted to Amy. She saw that the girl had grabbed on to the edge of a form-chair.

She turned back to the door, everything in slow motion now as the world shook—

—yet another monster scrabbled at the entry and Billie fired, blew it back. Strange, she had only seen its head—

She hiked herself up on one elbow and watched. The night was lit from the burning flier, monsters howled and ran past the doorway, the smell of burned materials gagged her—but—

Amy was alive.

It was her last thought before the darkness claimed her for itself.

The ship trembled as Ripley worked the lift controls. It rose at a slant, one of the mains out—but it did rise.

Fuck coordinates. Ripley grabbed the stick and

pushed, led the disabled ship up and away from
the creatures, headed west.

"Got 'em!" Tully shouted.

Wilks felt a grin spread across his face.

The *Kurtz* was in the air, flying an eight pattern
high over the compound. Wilks hadn't waited for
the bugs to show—half an hour into Ripley's time
limit, he'd had Brewster take the ship up. If they
were coming back, better that they had a clear
spot to land. . . .

Tully frowned. "Wait. It's not them—"

"Who else—?" Wilks began and then stopped.
He leaned over her shoulder and checked the
read. It was the other ship, the breeder. As he
watched, the vessel got closer to the compound
and started down—

"It's gonna crash," said Tully, her voice cracking.

It was them, it had to be, and they were about
to smack down hard. Wilks clenched his fists and
waited.

The ship was called the *Coleman*, according to
the control board. Odd how she would notice a
thing like that at a time like this. She navigated
the landscape as best she could, but the crippled
flier dipped and swayed alarmingly. She shouted
Billie's name once, but no answer. She had no
time to panic; alarm lights blinked across the console and told her that the flight would be a short
one.

They were almost to the compound when the blinking overheat panel turned to solid red.

"We're going down!" she called back. Sweat dripped from her scalp and she lowered the ship, prayed that the drop wouldn't kill them when the engines cut out.

The ship sheared off the tops of a dozen trees and hit the ground in a steep slide.

"Get down there, now!" said Wilks. His body felt tight and shaky as Brewster took the *Kurtz* down.

Billie opened her eyes as something shook her awake. She hurt all over, her stomach swam and dived—

Everything was strange, tilted. She sat up sideways and shook her head, wondered—

"Amy?" Her throat felt dry as sand.

The little girl clutched at a bolted chair across the room and wept. At the sound of Billie's voice, she lifted her puffy face and looked at her.

"Your daddy sent us," said Billie. "He's safe."

"Really?" Amy's eyes widened.

"Yes," said Billie. "Really."

Amy's face changed, the look of despair swept away. Tears still running, the child stood and stumbled across the room toward Billie, who stretched out her arms. Amy fell into them and hugged her hard.

Billie felt no pain, in spite of her wounds.

In fact, she'd never felt better in her whole life.

●   ●   ●

Ripley limped into the room and saw the two of them embracing. The sound of the *Kurtz*'s engines overhead was beautiful, a perfect complement to the picture before her.

"Let's get out of here," she said. Tears trickled down her cheeks for the first time in as long as she could remember.

She could still cry.

Something else to live for.

30

The *Kurtz* lifted, up through the atmosphere to where Orona's dish would be aimed. The dark Earth fell away.

Wilks stood at the door of medlab.

Billie and Ripley had both been wounded, but not as badly as he'd first thought when they'd staggered out of the ship. Both had acid burns, and Billie had inhaled a good amount of chemical smoke, but they were going to be okay. Jones checked the child for implantation; she was clean.

It was over. *Almost*, he amended.

He felt—pretty good, actually. For a change. The way Billie had smiled at him in medlab had something to do with it. . . .

He'd thought that the end would leave him empty, but it was having an opposite effect. There was still a lot of universe out there. He was old, yeah, but not dead yet.

Not by a long fucking shot. For a burnout, for a dumbass marine who had wasted so much of his life waiting for it to be over, he had finally done something worth doing—and now, he decided, it was time to move on.

Yeah.

Billie lay in her cot and felt sleepy and warm. Whatever Jones had given her was doing her a world of good.

Amy and her father had just left for the dining hall, hands linked. They'd sat on the exam table next to her for an hour, exchanged stories, paused now and then for pats and hugs. Amy cried through much of it; the emotional wounds would be slow to heal, Billie knew. But she would be there to help.

Billie felt a sense of peace that she had never felt before. The hiding was over. She had set out with the others little more than a scared child herself, had faced fears that had plagued her entire life—and had survived.

No, better. *They* had survived. Ripley, Wilks, Amy and her father, the rest—now they could move on.

To what, she didn't know—and as she felt consciousness slip away, she found she didn't care. There was love in her ... for Amy, for David— hard to think of him that way and not as Wilks, but she could get used to it. Things were okay—

Billie slept.

•   •   •

Ripley touched the plastiskin on her arm absently and stared into the blank computer. She sat in front of the controls, Tully, Wilks, and McQuade nearby.

Seeing Amy and Billie together had reminded her of a few things from her past, emotions that were real and strong, synthetic or not. She had played a part in the lives of these people; and she had discovered something in herself that she'd thought was gone forever—self-respect. She was ready to give a shit about who she was—*what* she was. Somehow, it wasn't nearly so frightening anymore. . . .

"Whenever you're ready," Tully said.

Ripley put her fingers on the keys; a sudden rush of energy flowed through her. What word could she type in, what word would tell the story best? It didn't matter, of course—any four-letter command on the right frequency would send the signal that began the countdown, the pulse that would start the clock running—but it felt important anyway, some symbolic gesture of the finality. . . .

After a moment, she tapped in the word *Life* and looked at it for a few seconds. Yes. That was appropriate.

With a steady hand, Ripley reached for the send key.

ABOUT THE AUTHOR

S. D. (STEPHANI DANELLE) PERRY writes multimedia novelizations in the fantasy/science fiction/horror genres for love and money. Besides several works in the *Aliens* universe, she has adapted the scripts for *Timecop* and *Virus* and written a *Xena, Warrior Princess* novel under the name Stella Howard. She also writes books based on video-games.

S. D. and her husband live in Portland, Oregon, with two sweet dogs and a rather nasty hedgehog named Miles.